The Bull

Matthew Weber

This book is dedicated to the two most important women in my life — my beautiful wife, Shanna, and my lovely mother, Diane. Thanks for your unending support and encouragement.

One thing about people from the South ... They do not like being told what to do.

The black Mustang blazed past the stop sign without a second's hesitation, barreling down the dark road like a stealth bomber on a mission. When he crested a hill where the trees cleared, Derek doused the headlights, rolled onto the grassy shoulder and cut the engine.

He crept onto the bridge as tandem balls of light streaked under his feet, only to vanish momentarily and emerge behind him as duets of fleeting red embers fading into the night. The interstate overpass was a whirl of bluster from the vehicles humming down the highway below.

He tied the first loop of twine to the concrete fence along the edge of the bridge, working feverishly and praying that no police cruisers rolled by on patrol.

He had collected several large plastic banners from a trash pile at the local ball park. The signs had lined the outfield fence, advertising various sponsors of the Fulton Springs Community Baseball League. After each season, the old signs were discarded so the baseball commission could solicit local businesses for new sponsorship. Derek had spray-painted over the artwork to prevent any color transmission and stenciled his message on the fresh, blank plastic of the other side.

Crouching behind the concrete columns to hide from the flashing headlights, he fumbled with the twine to thread its ends through the metal eyelets of the plastic sheet. He was glad to see that in relation to the size of the bridge that would support it, the width of his canvas and the stark simplicity of its message would make a boldly visible sign that was sure to get some notice —

Derek froze.

From the corner of his eye he saw the cruiser of a State Trooper move beneath the bridge like a shark on the hunt. His muscles stiffened. Had the cop seen him? The last thing he needed was more trouble with the authorities. He was on parole. Derek closed his eyes and said a little prayer. It seemed like a small eternity before the vehicle appeared on the other side of the bridge, gliding away with no indication of braking.

He released a pinched breath and returned to the task at hand.

The top of the banner was secured to the fence while the bottom was looped with heavy, lead plugs normally used for sinking deep-sea fishing lures. The weighted bottom would keep the sign taut and readable in the face of a stiff wind. The banner was 18 feet long, and Derek had centered it over the four southbound lanes of I-65 that ran through his home town of Fulton Springs, Alabama, and into the Birmingham metro area, where it would reach the thousands of

Monday morning commuters. As soon as the last eyelet was tied, he flipped the plastic over the bridge, working from one end to the other. The banner unfurled like a zipper and dropped tightly against the overpass to reveal blood-red letters against a plain white background.

The sign stated simply in giant block text: RESIST CONTROL.

Derek jogged across the bridge to his Mustang and cranked the engine. When he hit the street, he dropped the clutch and peeled out. As he tore down the road, purple light peeked over the pre-dawn horizon. He was an early riser, and those first rays of sunlight signified a special time of day for Derek. It was time for a bacon biscuit, and definitely coffee.

***

"Guinness, please," said Frank from behind the black lenses of his sunglasses. "Draft."

"Certainly, sir. Anything else?" asked the waiter.

"That'll do."

The waiter spun and trotted into the restaurant from the patio area.

On the concrete patio beneath his feet, Frank watched a cricket wriggling under the siege of several dozen red ants. The cricket appeared to be wounded, squirming and twitching. The cricket was several times larger and stronger than the ants, but the ants were vast in number and swarmed the cricket with their tiny, biting attacks until it was completely overwhelmed, and the ants feasted.

Frank Standish was sitting outside The Magnolia, a new restaurant and bar that opened a mere mile from Frank's own establishment, The Bull. Frank was owner, proprietor and often the bartender of The Bull and had carved himself a loyal niche of local patrons. The Magnolia had opened for business just a few days ago, and Frank was there to size up his competition.

The interior of the Magnolia was painted in turquoise and purple pastels and decorated with floral arrangements and contemporary abstract artwork that accented the colorful walls. The tall, high-backed chairs and stainless steel tables were brand new, as were the tile floor and the paneled ceiling. A lot of money had apparently been invested in the remodeling, and the bar had three times as many beers on tap as The Bull. Despite the flourishes, the place felt artificial to Frank, and a little flighty. Not his style, so he had decided on the patio.

He lit a cigarette, inhaling deeply and expelling a silky, serpentine cloud, enjoying the taste of the tobacco and the hypnotic movement of the slender plume of smoke as a light breeze pushed it away.

"Here you go, sir," said the waiter, returning with the mug of beer. "And, I'm sorry to be a bother, but you can't smoke here." The waiter was a thin, fey man in his early twenties with an ingratiating smile. He had black hair that was feathery in the back, long in the front, and frosted with violet highlights that curled sheepishly over his eyes. His shirt was two sizes too small.

"Can't smoke?" said Frank. He had a voice as dry as sandpaper. He sipped his beer.

"That's right, sir. No smoking. It's against the rules." The waiter was all smiles.

Frank glassed the kid up and down. "I'm seated outdoors," he said as he exhaled a pale gray puff that drifted briefly toward the waiter and vanished.

"Yes, sir. Still, it's against the law. It's a new city ordinance we were given as soon as we opened for business. The city considers the patio part of our dining area, so no smoking."

Frank examined the other patrons of the Magnolia's patio. A bookish man in a suit pecked intently at a laptop computer. An attractive young couple made goo-goo eyes at each other over a plate of vegetarian nachos. Two elderly women were sipping mimosas. None were smoking, and the two women were glaring at him with cold judgment.

"Where am I supposed to smoke?" asked Frank, leaning his elbow against the wrought-iron rail at his side. This was the first he had heard of this fresh ripple in the city's ever-expanding cigarette policy. Frank was not exactly a staunch enforcer of such regulations at The Bull, but it was smart to stay on top of which laws he was breaking.

The waiter pointed to the sidewalk directly on the other side of the black rail where Frank was leaning.

"The sidewalk's okay with us," said the waiter. Frank's frown unsettled him.

"It's okay to smoke right there ... but not here?"

Frank rubbed the bridge of his nose, restraining his exasperation. It had been a long morning. He stubbed out the butt on the calloused palm of his hand.

"Well, you can still be ticketed by the cops for smoking on the sidewalk," said the waiter, "but it's not our responsibility to enforce." He flashed a paper-thin smile and twirled back into the restaurant.

Frank took two heavy swigs of beer, soaking in the rich taste of the stout, and turned his attention to the menu. The Magnolia offered such progressive delicacies as Fritto Misto, which was described as fried squash blossoms and mushrooms stuffed with a mixture of vegan cream cheese, shallots, nutritional yeast, salt and pepper. Also served was mushroom and pea risotto with grilled tofu. One of the house specialties was the coconut curry crepe stuffed with eggplant. Once a week from 6 to 8 PM the Magnolia was to host Raw Food Wednesday "for the best in simplistic nutritional dining." He closed the menu.

He pulled out the cigarette pack and slapped it against his palm, packing the tobacco. His eyes fell to the cricket carcass covered with ants. He stamped it flat, grinding the ants into the concrete. Frank walked around the railing and stood not two feet away from where he had been sitting. He smoked his cigarette, politely puffing away from the patio area while sipping his beer.

The waiter returned and approached Frank timidly. "Sir, I really do not mean to be a burden, but I'm afraid you aren't allowed to consume alcohol on the sidewalk."

Frank was a tall, broad man in his fifties with a mane of salt and pepper hair, a stony visage and a thick silver moustache that he wore like a sheriff's badge. He was dressed in his usual faded blue jeans and black leather jacket. He cocked his head to the side. "What?" he said flatly.

The waiter fluttered his eyes uncertainly and put his palms in the air. "I don't make the rules, sir."

"So, I can drink there," said Frank, pointing to the chair on the patio, "but not *here?*" he said, pointing at his feet just inches from the chair.

"And I can smoke here," he said, releasing a cloud from his lips. "But not *there* ..."

"Yes, sir."

"Even though I'm basically standing in the same place?" asked Frank.

"Sounds silly, I know." To the waiter, Frank looked like some sort of cowboy who had joined a motorcycle gang. "You're drinking a beer you purchased from us, so the city holds us responsible."

"What if it wasn't a beer from your place?"

The waiter shrugged. "You could still go to jail for public consumption, but it wouldn't be our problem—just yours and the cops'."

Frank's head hurt. He took off his sunglasses and squinted at the boy incredulously. "Does that make any sense to you, son?"

The waiter dropped his head and shook it. "Not really. But we're trying not to make a fuss. Me and my—my friend—we're trying to get the place off the ground. It's our first shot at our own business. Being new in town, we're trying not to cause a stir, you know?"

Frank was learning exactly what he had hoped to learn. Two things gave him a surge of confidence over his new rival in the bar scene. First, the Magnolia evidently targeted an entirely different type of clientele than did The Bull. And second, the Magnolia was going to follow The Rules. Let the chips fall where they may.

***

Frank unlocked the door of the Bull and sifted through the day's mail. As expected, he found a letter from the city explaining how the new smoking ordinance must be applied to his business. If Frank had thought that making his restaurant an entirely non-smoking establishment would help his business, then The Bull would already be a non-smoking establishment. Only a couple miles away, both north and south, there were bars outside of Fulton Springs that were not hindered with the same restrictions. When patrons could no longer smoke at The Bull, they would go to the other bars where they could smoke in comfort. It was the simple cause-and-effect of a free market, only Frank's end of the market was no longer as free as his competition's.

Frank hated The Rules, and fought them every chance he got. In Fulton Springs, The Rules were always changing at the behest of Mayor Davenport Cornelius, known as Reverend Dave to his supporters, but known as That Fat Jackass to Frank and most of the patrons at The Bull. Mayor Cornelius justified his legal edicts with the wag of a Bible and claims for the betterment of society, a tactic endorsed by his loyal city council. The council consisted largely of the deacons of the First Baptist Church of Fulton Springs, the local mega-church where Cornelius had presided before stepping down for the sake of his political pursuits. And, although he was no longer technically the leader of the church, everyone recognized that he was still the unspoken man in charge, choreographing the pageantry at the Sunday podium.

During his first term as mayor, Cornelius managed to pass many new laws for the "betterment of society," beginning with an increase in business taxes to fund new computers for high school students. That was passed in his first year in office, and reportedly four PCs had since been purchased for the high school, thanks to the tens of thousands of dollars of increased annual tax revenue. The official City of Fulton Springs website described the initial expenditure as "an exploratory first step in the program." Frank doubted that even the four computers existed. In essence, the new law meant The Bull—and all of Fulton Springs business owners—lost money as Cornelius and company gained it. And since the city council was responsible for budgetary oversight, nobody in charge raised a stink.

The tax hike struck Frank as a thinly veiled ruse for the city to grab cash, and he made some quick enemies at the council meetings. Thanks to his grousing, a number of the town's other business owners grew increasingly aware of the shenanigans. However, they felt they had to whisper in the shadows. Those who suspected the mayor and council of dirty dealings were silenced by fear of being portrayed as greedy Scrooges who would deny children an important means of modern education for the sake of retaining more of their selfish profit. Gossip spread quickly at First Baptist, and it seemed that half the city went to that church. Nobody could afford to lose the business.

One of Cornelius's recent missions was to roll back the legal business hours of drinking establishments. Formerly, the doors of The Bull had been open until 2 AM each morning. The new law mandated closing the doors at midnight. The mayor's justification was that the law would save lives by discouraging drunken driving.

Coincidentally, a lobbying group in favor of alcohol prohibition had recently contributed generously to the mayor's campaign coffers.

Frank protested the law at a city council meeting. He cited the city's own public records showing the incidence of drunken driving had decreased by roughly 40 percent over the previous three years, when his late-night hours had been up and running.

"But we can do better," was the reply given off-handedly by one of the council members, a round man in a cheap suit with ketchup on his tie.

"We already have laws against driving while intoxicated," said Frank. "Why don't you enforce the laws we have rather than passing new laws that obstruct my ability to do business." He argued that driving drunk was a crime unto itself and should be pursued on an individual case-by-case basis rather than limiting the lifestyle choices of everyone else in town, the vast majority of whom had not been found guilty of that particular traffic offense. He made the point that legally mandating when and where people could do what they wanted to do was nothing more than inhibiting their freedom of choice and discouraging personal responsibility. He was told that indeed both the old and new laws would be enforced, for the betterment of the people of Fulton Springs and society at large. The law was passed.

The busiest hours for The Bull fell during the late shift. The new law hit the business right in its bottom line, mandating a 20-percent reduction in its current operating hours. Naturally, Frank ignored the command until the police showed up to enforce compliance.

Next, the mayor introduced prohibition on Sundays. Sunday was the Lord's Day after all, explained Cornelius, and should be respected as such. Frank was a long-time believer, but he was also a freedom-loving businessman. He voiced a stern but reverent protest at the council meeting, but it was explained to him that prohibiting drinking on Sundays encouraged more family time and church attendance, which was better for the community and society as a whole. Frank stormed out of the meeting, resisting the urge to wag his middle finger in the air behind him. Frank could serve food on Sundays, but his popular and profitable Bloody Mary Sunday Brunch had been sacrificed on the altar of piety.

Over and over, Frank begrudgingly endured the body blows to his business model. New taxes. New restrictions. New permits required. But he was hardening. His reluctance to succumb to the ever-expanding edicts was increasing. For him, the deeply rooted notion that this was "just the way things were" in Fulton Springs was deteriorating. Government intrusion too often seemed an inescapable fact of life, one of fate's many trials to overcome, like a physical malady or a disastrous flood. But at the local level, that sense was waning for Frank.

One evening two young men came into The Bull, greeting the patrons with beaming smiles, shaking their hands and distributing leaflets promoting the reelection of Mayor Davenport Cornelius. They walked to the bar where young Derek was cleaning up. When they recognized him they stopped their approach. Derek locked eyes with the two and dropped his towel. The last time he had encountered these dapper, turtle-necked former classmates, a few heated words were exchanged, and then things had turned violent.

"Boss, you've got company," called Derek, staring them up and down warily. He felt a tingle at the back of his neck. He instinctively made a fist.

So did the other two.

Frank stepped out of the kitchen. "What can I do for you?" The double saloon doors swung loosely behind him. A cigarette hung from the corner of his mouth.

The young men spun to greet him with gratified smiles, happy to avoid Derek. They introduced themselves—Pierce Mathers and Billy Farling—and requested to post the campaign flyers on the walls of the restaurant, inside and out.

Frank knew of these kids. His policy at The Bull was generally *come one, come all*, an open invitation to just about anyone and everyone who darkened the door. In fact, painted on the glass of the front door were the words, *Everyone is Welcome (unless you're not)*. The mayor and his lackeys provided the exception. He recognized one of the boys as the newest and youngest face on the Fulton Springs city council—a big strike against him. The other was the son of a cop.

Frank glared at the two boys with a loathsome coldness that wilted their plastic smiles. He gave a clear and concise command: "Get the hell out of my restaurant."

They shrunk like dying flowers.

"But … wait … What's the deal?" stammered Mathers, who could not understand why their glad-handing had not worked its magic. "All we'd like to do is put up these flyers for Reverend Dave—I mean, Mayor Cornelius. As a business man, I thought you'd appreciate all the Mayor has done for the people of Fulton Springs."

"Get out of here." Frank was an oak.

"Can we speak to your supervisor?"

"I own The Bull, and you and your flyers are not welcome here." He took a step toward them.

Billy Farling stuffed the leaflets back into his duffle bag. "Let's get out of here."

"Fine!" said Mathers, slinking toward the door.

Frank: "And tell That Fat Jackass you call a boss that he's not welcome around here, either." He eyeballed them out of The Bull, in case they required further encouragement to leave. They did not.

The door swung closed.

"Way to tell 'em, Pop," said Derek.

Later that evening a Fulton Springs police officer stopped by The Bull to issue Frank a $500 citation for smoking in a prohibited area—his restaurant.

***

The Bull's bar was thick with smoke.

"I've had it. I'm fed up," said Selby Warner, staring at the televised nightly newscast. "I mean, come tax season I'll be staring down the same loaded gun I do every year when the government skins me alive, and all the while I'm hearing on TV about the bigwig Wall Street execs who are skirtin' away with billions of taxpayer dollars … the same dollars that working men like myself have to cough up out of our hard-earned paychecks. And the government's just as bad, if not worse. Spending us right into the third world. I fear for my grandkids. It just ain't right."

Selby tilted the bottle of beer to his whiskery mug and chugged down a few hearty gulps. He lifted his finger theatrically and professed in an affected display of pseudo-sophistication to any bar patron who bothered to listen: "Do not ask for whom the bell tolls … on tax day, it tolls for thee … and *me*," he hiccupped. Selby was a fixture at The Bull, living just two blocks away, easy stumbling distance. Frank would never let him drive drunk, so Selby moved to an apartment closer to The Bull. He was sixty-six years old, a self-employed plumber and a Vietnam veteran. He had a saddlebag face and swollen red eyes. He turned to the bar and said, "One day I'd like to have enough money holed away to retire. Know what I mean, Frank?"

Frank lifted his eyes from his newspaper. He wordlessly gave a thumbs-up to Selby, who continued his litany of grievances.

"… But the people in charge, they sure don't make it easy … Then, on the other hand, you have all these jackasses who vote the idiots into office, hopin' they can get somethin' for nothin'. Lookin' for a government handout. A free lunch. That handout is the *tax payers'* money. We *earned* it. The politicians take it, and give it to whoever votes them into office. It's a helluva vicious circle. It's the same damn problem we got here in town. Hell, I go to work, get scalped by taxes, and still pay my bills, even if it means I'm eating' beans all month. 'Cause that's how we built this country. Hard work! Not by dependin' on the government to do the providin'." Selby killed his Budweiser. "Ain't that right, Frank?"

Frank didn't look up from his paper but only nodded robotically. He was one of the few polite enough to respond, albeit aloofly, to Selby's unfocused nightly tirades.

"Who pays the government's bills, Frank? And who gets hung out to dry?"

"We pay 'em, Selby," said Frank indifferently, concentrating on a crossword puzzle in the dim light of the bar. "The taxpayer gets hung out to dry." A common refrain.

"Right … You're right about that."

Rocky Jones' perspiring face appeared from the kitchen through the expedite window behind the bar. "Ribs up!" he shouted as he dropped a plate of fresh, steaming, sauce-laden baby backs on the counter. Frank grabbed the plate and slid it to Selby, who dove in with ravenous vigor.

The Bull was an old, gray cedar-sided building with interior cinder-block walls painted crimson and adorned with a hodgepodge of barroom regalia, from neon signs and autographed football jerseys to dart boards, a couple of mounted lake bass and lots of novelty signs, which boasted such witticisms as: *That Which Hits the Fan Will Not Be Evenly Distributed.*

Entertainment highlights included a CD-playing jukebox, a pool table and a vintage pinball machine promoting the rock band, KISS. Also available were a dartboard, a foosball table and two electronic slot machines. The slot machines were usually co-piloted by Frieda Collins and Betsy Willingham, elderly but feisty Catholic ladies who relished their change-purse gambling.

One corner of the barroom served as a shrine dedicated to Frank's younger years as a leading auto racer on the Alabama dirt-track circuit, featuring photographs and trophies from the glory days. The tables in that particular corner were the understood territory of a small pack of bikers, helmed by the Butler brothers, Buck and Bobby, all beards, beer guts and bad attitudes on the outside, but with soft, gooey centers beneath all the black leather.

The Bull's barbecue drew people from many counties away to the sweet, savory spice of Rocky's prize-winning special sauce and his legendary finesse with slow-roast grilling. The dining lobby offered a dozen mismatched tables and folding chairs and was partitioned to provide a dedicated smoking section. However, the new city ordinance completely banned all smoking in any establishment that was open to the public. The Bull was in violation.

The nightly regulars crowded around the large, shellacked oak bar at the front of the restaurant, below the cool glow of two ceiling-mounted television sets. Mounted over the bar was The Bull's *pièce de résistance*—a huge steer skull with broad, thick horns.

From one of the televisions Frank overheard a snippet of a newscast that drew his attention. On the screen he saw the Fulton Springs bridge that crossed I-65. The camera angle was slowly zooming on a sign dangling from the bridge, where the message could easily be read. Frank turned up the volume.

"*—the sign has since been removed by police,*" reported the local female newscaster, Daphne Shields. "*Authorities have requested that Channel 13 News remind our viewers that it is unlawful to post advertisements—political or otherwise—on a public right of way without the proper permits.*"

"What's that about?" barked Selby, pointing to the TV with one hand as he scooted his bar stool closer with the other. "I saw that sign on the drive into work this mornin'. 'Resist Control' is what it said."

"Sounds like you know everything they do," said Frank.

"Do they know who did it?"

Frank shrugged. "I didn't hear. I don't think so."

"I saw that thing this mornin' and thought *hell, yeah!*—that's what I've been *talkin' about*," said Selby. "The people need to get angry and rise up when the government gets too big for our own good. That's what this country was founded on. We need some people to rattle the cage."

"A sign?" inserted Derek from across the room as he bussed dishes from the dining tables. "What good does a sign do, anyway?"

"A sign does a lot of good. It gets people thinkin'," said Selby. "Signs are used to sell things. And to sell ideas. And look, that sign got noticed by the Channel 13 News."

"And we're talking about it right now," added Frank.

Derek racked some glasses. "Yeah, I guess we are talking about it." Nice publicity, he thought.

***

"I don't understand!" said Mayor Cornelius. "What's the holdup?" He drummed his sausage fingers over the development plans that lay across his desk, a blueprint for the anticipated Fulton Springs Galleria. The Galleria was a shopping center in the early stages of construction between I-65 and Highway 31, complete with a new interstate exit. It would boast 22 new retail establishments along with a predicted 1.3 million dollars in annual tax revenue, once everything was up and running. This was Cornelius's most ambitious city project to date, but there was a hitch.

"It's the Stonewall residence, sir," said Pierce Mathers, the young councilman who the mayor had come to consider his right-hand man. "He doesn't want to budge. Mr. Stonewall's a stubborn old codger who said there wasn't enough money in the whole state to buy him out of his home. He had some rather unsavory words for you as well, sir."

Although Pierce was not one of Reverend Dave's First Baptist flock, the boy had mounted his own campaign for a council seat right out of college, aggressively publicizing his name throughout town with a canvas of campaign signs. The Fulton Springs citizens had lazily voted him into office solely on the basis of name recognition, due to all the signs. The mayor had been impressed with Pierce's youthful initiative and found his political intuition a useful tool.

Although popular in school, Pierce had barely cut it as a small town wide receiver and had no talent for a college football career. It was clear upon high school graduation that a future in sports was not on the table, so in college he set his site on politics, which he viewed as a competition of popularity that paid rewards in power and influence. Another class election.

"That ornery ol' cuss has always been a pain in the ass," said Reverend Dave. He slumped behind his huge mahogany desk, stroking his chins pensively. "What are our options? Doesn't the city have a right to seize the house based on eminent domain?"

"Well, sir," said Pierce, clearing his throat in an effort to sound authoritative on the subject, "in the Kelo case back in 2005, the Supreme Court ruled 5 to 4 that the Fifth Amendment's takings clause did not prevent the city of New London—that's in Connecticut—from taking Suzette Kelo's home for the expressed purpose of private development in order to gain increased tax revenue."

"'Did *not* prevent' … That sounds good. Hell, that's gangbusters," said the reverend. "Cut him a shut-up check and then throw the man out. We've got our justification."

"I wish we could, sir, but it's just not that simple."

The mayor let out a long sigh. "And why, pray tell, is that?"

"It turns out that in the wake of the Kelo case, Alabama was actually the first state to enact new protections against local governments seizing property for private enterprise. In other words, right after the Feds gave us the green light, the state clipped our wings."

Cornelius's face furrowed into a Chinese Shar Pei. "This is not information that I want to hear today, Piercey. I don't want to hear what we *can't* do. I want to hear what we *have the power* to do."

Pierce hated being called *Piercey*. "One option is to build a public right-of-way through the property," he said. "That way we could argue that we're seizing the property for public domain, rather than for private interests. Maybe a road that connects Walker Avenue to Highway 31. Of course, we'd have to pretty much scrap the current development plans and redraw the whole thing." Pierce thumped the sprawling paperwork covering the mayor's desk.

"That won't work. The investors are sticklers for what they've got drawn up, and I already assured them that we were in the clear. They might bail if I approach them with drastic changes. That requires way too much red tape and revenue that I don't have at my disposal. I ain't got that kind of time, Piercey!"

Pierce walked to the corner of the room and poured himself a refill of sugar with a little coffee. He stood sipping, looking out the office window. He had something up his sleeve but wanted to draw out the mayor's anguish, so when he proposed his solution it would sound even sweeter, win him more favor.

Cornelius rubbed his temples. "I don't guess there's any chance Stonewall's going to keel over from a bad heart any time soon?"

"Sure, there's a *chance,* sir. He's old as dirt."

Cornelius pounded his fist. "Dammit … so much for sure bets. I do not have this kind of time." The mayor wadded a napkin into a ball and plopped it into his empty Styrofoam coffee cup.

"Well, there *is* an exception to the law," said Pierce in a futile effort not to sound coy. He stood silently as if in deep pontification.

"Yeah? Well, spit it out!"

"I'm not sure if we can hang our hats on it, but we can legally take over the property for private interest if, and only if, we can prove the property is blighted. If it's dangerous—something like that—then there's a loophole in the law."

"Are you kidding? Of course it's dangerous. That house is ancient, and falling down around the old man. I deem the Stonewall property blighted!" the mayor slammed his fist. "Can I do that?"

"I'll look into it, sir." Inside the straight line of his mouth, Pierce was grinning from ear to ear.

***

The door of The Bull creaked open, allowing a splash of afternoon sunlight to illuminate the dimness as an elderly man hobbled in with the help of cane. He had a bent and shrunken frame but he ambled determinedly straight to the bar and saddled himself onto a stool. Frank poured the man his daily stein of Pabst Blue

Ribbon and placed it in front of him.

"Afternoon, Oscar."

"Howdy, Frank," greeted Oscar Stonewall, "How's the family?" He asked this every day.

"Peachy," said Frank. "You should see Nora in her costume for the school play. They're putting on 'The Tortoise and the Hare' and she got the part of the tortoise. Her costume's got a tail and a cardboard shell—the works."

Oscar smiled. "I'll bet she's as cute as a little red wagon going up a hill," he said. "And the boy?"

Frank wiped off the bar top with a towel. "Staying out of trouble these days," he said.

"Heck of a carpenter, your son," nodded Oscar.

"He's also been pulling some shifts here at the bar to earn some extra dough. Going to school, too. He's got his head on straight."

"My, my ... that sounds fine, real fine," said Oscar. "You don't see that kind of work ethic in too many kids these days. How 'bout Fancy? How is she?"

"The wife is well," he said, as he toweled off some freshly washed beer mugs. "She's working on one of her sculptures right now. A commissioned deal. Should be making a good chunk of change once it's complete. I'll tell her you said hello."

"That's nice." Oscar tipped the beer to his lips and let out a satisfied sigh. "I think it's great that she can do something she loves and make money at it. Most people can't marry those two things—work and pleasure. Only the lucky few."

Frank racked the glasses. "Lucky? Maybe a little. But she waited a lot of tables for a lot of years before she made her name as an artist. She had a long climb to get where she is."

"Even better!" Oscar, raising his stein in salute.

"How 'bout you, Oscar? What's new?"

The old man's face darkened as he scratched his shiny bald head. "Nothing new. Same old crap," his tone lowered. "Getting grief from the city about my house holding up 'progress.' I guess some men have a different view of what 'progress' means, and me and the mayor don't see eye to eye."

Frank shook his head. "That mayor's a piece of work."

Oscar's mood could turn on a nail head. He gazed into the mirror behind the multicolored bottles of liquor that adorned the bar shelves and saw a weary and wilted but still headstrong man gaze back. "I don't see why everybody's got to be in such a damn hurry all the time," he said. "These days everybody's always rushing around, moving and shaking, chasing a dollar. Never settling down and enjoying a good conversation. That's why I like this place. It's relaxing."

Frank filled a bowl of pretzels for Oscar.

"But those damn city big-wigs are so hot to change things, whether old timers like myself agree with it or not. It makes a fella feel tired, with them always trying to lean on me, doing everything but grabbin' me up and tossin' me in the street. I get a knock on the door once or twice a week offering me just a pittance more money to move out. And the phone calls ... Hell, the phone calls come every day, and nobody says nothin', I just hear breathing on the line. I reckon they're tryin' to spook me, but I don't spook too easy."

"Good for you, Oscar. Stand your ground."

"They got rid of Esther Castleberry, though. The poor thing. She's a 74-year old widow, been living there for 30 years, and they run her off with all the harassment. She couldn't take it. She moved in with her daughter in Shelby County."

Frank grimaced. He didn't know Esther well, but had heard that the woman was being pressured by the city because she sat on prime shopping mall property. He hated that she felt forced to relinquish her home.

"But I ain't leaving," said Oscar. "I mean, hell, I'm 84 years old. I doubt I got too many days left. They can wait me out. When I'm dead and gone, they can level the place and build their damn shopping center however they want. But not 'til then. Everybody's just in such a hurry, it's shameful."

With another burst of light, the front door opened and Sharon McClendon sauntered into the bar, shuffling her car keys deep into her oversized purse. As usual, she was wearing too much makeup and too short a skirt for a woman pushing fifty, but she had a soft and honest smile that could warm a can of soup. She sat right next to Oscar, pulled her stool closer and planted a kiss on his cheek. "How you doing, buddy?"

"I just got a lot better," said Oscar.

"Iced tea?" asked Frank.

"Iced tea will be fine, Mr. Frank," said Sharon with a ruby red smile. "That'd be perfect."

"'Perfect' ..." repeated Oscar. "I like the way you say 'perfect', Sharon."

Oscar had a crush on Sharon.

***

Pierce Mathers and Billy Farling stood outside Oscar Stonewall's house. Pierce held a note pad and pen, and Billy concealed a Budweiser in a Burger King cup.

"We're supposed to find out what's wrong with the old guy's house, right?" said Billy.

Pierce didn't answer. He began jotting notes regarding any apparent signs of "blight" that he could see. The roof was sagging—*check*. Probably structurally unsound and unsafe, he speculated without the hindrance of any actual knowledge of building practices. The concrete front steps were crumbling, an obvious threat to foot traffic—*check*. The brick paver sidewalk was uneven and deteriorated, and wrought with roots and weeds. Someone could trip and fall—*check*. The shabby roof shingling surely had some leaks, which can cause serious water damage and serve as a breeding ground for the dreaded black mold, a known health hazard—*check*. The cracked and taped single-pane windows were likely to shatter at any moment, sending lethal shards of glass flying into the necks and eyes of passing children—*check*. And shudder to think what ghastly discoveries were certain to lie unseen behind the closed doors. This was a goldmine of blight if ever there was one. Pierce bristled with excitement at the prospect of delivering the good news to Mayor Cornelius. His burgeoning political future was looking bright, indeed.

"Crappy paint job, for starters," said Billy.

***

The Bull was more abuzz than usual when Frank walked through the door to relieve Derek's afternoon bartending shift.

"There's Frank!" shouted Selby, spinning on his barstool. He bounded across the bar, his excitement boiling over. "Tell him about it, Oscar. Tell him about this bullcrap! Frank, you won't believe this—typical big government bullyin' from That Fat Jackass in office. It's ridiculous! Tell him, Oscar!"

Everyone was gathered around Oscar who was slumped over the bar with his head in his hands. Sharon was kneading the muscles of his neck, massaging him in consolation.

"Cornelius has done it again, Pop," said Derek. "Listen to this…"

Oscar lifted his head, visibly depleted. "They're kicking me out," he croaked. "I thought I had rights. I don't. They're sending me packing, right out of my own home."

Frank was stunned. He stood frozen for a moment. Everyone waited for his reaction in rapt anticipation. They knew he was a seasoned vet when it came to battling the city.

"They can't do that," said Frank. "You own the place outright. We have laws."

"They found some sort of loophole," said Derek. "They're categorizing his house as 'blight.' Read this." He thrust the official notice into his father's hands, secretly hoping to elicit a justifiably fierce reaction. Maybe Frank would throw a bar stool, or punch a wall, let fly a string of profanity. Derek was an angry young man and longed for any exhibition of palpable rage with which he could identify and feel a kinship with his dad.

Frank looked down and scoured the letter. As he read line by line, he began to fume. It was yet another of the strong-arm tactics he'd grown to expect from Cornelius. According to city government, the property was deemed unfit for occupancy. There was a long list of mandated renovations, everything from structural repairs to new roofing, window replacement, landscaping requirements and more that required completion in order to comply with new city codes. The demands would require thousands of dollars in labor and materials, which was money Oscar Stonewall simply did not have.

"They've got me bent over a barrel, Frank," said Oscar. "I can't afford the work, and they know it good and well." Oscar's eyes were red and watery, the sight of which sent a current of fury coursing through Frank.

"This is downright evil." Frank slammed the letter onto the bar. "I'm sorry, Oscar."

"What're we gonna do, Frank?" asked Selby. "We always take care of our own here at The Bull. We can't let 'em sweep Oscar away, right out of his house. We gotta knock some heads ... stick it to The Man."

"How much time do we have to comply with the ordinance?" asked Frank.

Derek peeked at the letter. "Thirty days," he said.

"Thirty days ..." repeated Frank. "Thirty days to fix up that house, at the cost of an arm and a leg. What kind of preacher kicks an old man out of his house?"

"Maybe we oughtta burn down city hall," slurred Selby. Nobody paid him any attention.

Frank marched to the far end of the pub and looked out the window that led onto Main Street. Cars cruised by cautiously on streets slick from a drizzling rain. He looked out this window every day. The steady pace of the intersecting traffic strumming along day after day was like the heartbeat of their small town. The heartbeat but not the heart, which lay with the people. The people were the heart of the community, and their freedom its breath of life, thought Frank. The people mattered more than shopping malls. The city's priorities seemed all out of whack.

As Frank contemplated, a stray silver cat appeared through the glass beneath the window, hovering beneath the building overhang to seek shelter from the falling rain. It paused to lick itself clean. Frank had seen a lot of that cat recently. It was fond of the barbecue scraps that Rocky not-so-secretly piled on a plate for it outside the dumpster. The cat looked at Frank and momentarily held his gaze, cocking its head curiously. The cat then turned away and crept down the sidewalk, prowling intently in the direction of city hall.

"I'm sick of them pushing everyone around," said Frank. "Why can't they just leave everyone the hell alone?"

Frank stroked his iron moustache, eyes aimed in the direction of that lonesome silver cat.

"You got any ideas, Pop?"

Frank's patience was threadbare. He could endure the licks the city kept dishing out, but he would not abide them leaning on his friends.

"There's only one idea worth having," said Frank. "We fight for what's right."

Derek nodded, satisfied with his father's conviction. "Right on, Pop!"

***

Frank had a brutal migraine by the time he got home, a sharp, pulsing pain right behind the eyeballs that pounded his brain like a gas-driven piston. He chased a headache powder with a pint of water and collapsed onto the sofa in his living room. Fancy arose from the hallway and climbed beside him, sliding her fingers onto his shoulders and massaging the muscles along his neck. He melted, his rocky demeanor softening with each calming caress of her hand.

"Hi, baby," she said, her voice like silk, "I heard you had a bad day."

He reached up and touched her hand. "I guess you talked to Derek."

"He told me what happened to Oscar," she said. "It's a shame. Poor ol' guy shouldn't have to put up with this mess." She wore a satin champagne nightgown that accentuated her smooth, dark skin.

"Everyone at the bar is turning to me for some sort of solution." He kissed her and gave her a worried look.

"Of course they are. They always do. You're like a hero to them." She smiled and curled up on the couch, placing her head on his lap. "Frank 'the Bull' Standish, racing legend and the Grand Poobah of their favorite hangout. 'Heavy is the head that wears the crown.'"

He switched on the television and surfed the channels with the volume muted, searching for some lightweight diversion as he unwound for the night. With Fancy at his side, he could finally relax, tension fading, headache subsiding. She had an uncanny way of making that happen.

"I don't want a crown," said Frank. "But the reverend does. That's the problem. I just want everyone to leave each other alone. Let people live their lives the way they see fit. That goes for us, and for Oscar. For the people at the bar. For everyone."

"Well, maybe it's time that someone took that crown away from Mayor Davenport Cornelius. Maybe it's time someone put that office to better use."

Frank's head was still swimming with a stew of bitter

thoughts and spikes of anger. Fulton Springs was not a kingship after all, but for years no viable candidate had challenged the powerful Reverend, and the local elections always felt like foregone conclusions. Who would replace him? Among Frank's friends and patrons, there was plenty of griping to go around but never any proactive attempt to change their lot in life. There seemed to exist a grim sense of inevitability that things would always remain the way they were—or get worse—and aspiring for anything more was a pointless waste of time and energy. As long as Cornelius was around, everyone would do things Cornelius's way. The mayor had every election sewn up with the backing of the big church, which led to a sense of helplessness among the voters who disagreed with his policies. That sense of helplessness guaranteed the status quo. People disengaged from the process, and their resulting apathy to city leadership shackled any drive to change the very governing body that caused their distress. Like anyone in an unchecked seat of power, the mayor welcomed the disinterest of his detractors and grew fat from it. But as the government got fatter, it also got hungrier and was becoming unstoppable. It was like a nightmare octopus, with many arms swinging in many different directions, grabbing everything it could to fuel its ever-growing size.

Frank had unconsciously stopped changing the channels, with the television landing on the image of an on-location reporter who appeared, through her muted report, to be covering some sort of local human interest story on dogs and cats. Probably another story on the Humane Society, thought Frank. In a humane society, would an old man be ousted from his house in favor of another Shoe Depot?

The image of that reporter burned into his mind. Frank had an idea.

***

Oscar was engrossed in his work, intensely whittling a dry chunk of wood into the shape of a tortoise—a gift for Nora Standish. His hobby was practically a perpetual activity, whether he was watching television or just sitting on his front porch watching the traffic, he was always carving something—an animal, a plane, a train, figurines—and hundreds of the finished statuettes populated his house, adorning every shelf, mantle, table or virtually any available flat surface.

Oscar's quiet little acts of creation were escapism as much as anything else. His wife had passed away from cancer twenty years earlier. His son had died in an auto accident. His daughter was married and lived on the West Coast, but she had no children and kept in touch with him less and less as time went by. He was a lonely man, but carving kept him focused and forgetful of his loneliness. He would gather his wood from two sizeable chestnut trees in his backyard, dry it in his shed until it was ripe, then saw it into sections and rough-shape it to a workable size with a drawknife. He would then impart the detail with carving knives, parting tools, files and gouges—always hand tools, never electric. He lost himself in the process, enjoying the development of his vision, inhabiting all the grooves and fine cuts that breathed life to the shape.

Today was different. He felt a subtle buzzing in his ear, like a damaged transformer before it explodes atop a power pole. He could not shake it. He swatted at his ears but it was no help. He was not hearing the buzz; he was thinking it. It was a warning alarm that he refused to recognize, the irrefutable knowledge that his days at home were numbered. He bent over his tortoise and carved faster, shaving little bits of wood into a wispy pile at the foot of his rocking chair. His hands, crooked and cavernous, ached with arthritis, but he carried on. He thumped the wood with the blade, taking pleasure in the tapping sound that momentarily overpowered the buzzing in his head. He ran his fingers over the shape, enjoying the contours he was developing. His hands moved feverishly, flying in a robotically inhuman fashion. He cursed the buzzing, which seemed to grow louder and louder. He slashed at the wooden figurine wildly, hacking now rather than carving and abandoning any pretense of precision. He drew back the knife, swept it forward and sunk the blade deeply into the meat of his palm.

The tortoise fell. Its legs broke off. A hot flash of pain ripped up his arm, and he pulled the wounded hand into his flannel shirt to avoid dripping blood all over the house as he ambled inside from the porch to find a towel. He would have to walk to the Emergency Care Center two miles up the road but at least, he reasoned, he had something new to occupy his mind and replace that buzzing.

***

"Hi, this is Daphne Shields, reporter for Channel 5's 'Community Heartbeat.' I'm returning a call to Mr. Standish," said the business-like voice on the phone.

"This is Frank Standish. I appreciate you getting back to me."

"You're welcome. You had mentioned that you had a possible human interest story for the show."

Frank explained Oscar Stonewall's property plight very

matter-of-factly, detailing the city's stated intent to foreclose his property without explicitly personalizing Cornelius as the villainous mastermind—that was a conclusion he hoped the television audience would draw on its own.

"That is a shame, but it could be a potentially divisive story," she said warily. "That kind of thing generally makes my editor skittish, when there's the chance for community backlash. Sad as it is to say, there may be a lot of residents who side with the city, particularly if there's a legitimate complaint that the property is blighted or dangerous in any way."

"But I've got a positive spin for you, ma'am." Frank had anticipated her reluctance. As a news provider, the network needed to appear objective and avoid making political enemies unless there was an extremely good reason. "This will really tug at the heartstrings. The story's not about the foreclosure—that's a bummer. The story's about a community that comes together, with everybody pitching in, to fix up the old guy's house so he can keep living there. I've got a whole crew volunteering, mostly folks who know Mr. Stonewall from hanging around the restaurant I own—The Bull."

"Wait a minute," she said, sorting through a mental file cabinet. "You're Frank 'the Bull' Standish?"

"That's me, one and the same. You've heard of me?"

Her memory reeled back to childhood. "My father was a fan. He took me to see a couple of your races when I was a kid."

"Well, I'm glad. It's nice to be remembered."

"I think you're right about the story, Mr. Standish."

"Call me Frank."

"Local volunteers to the rescue ... That's always a heart-warmer, and we get to feature a local celebrity to boot."

Frank could hear her smile, and did the same. "I hardly think

I'm a celebrity."

"I'll have to run the idea past my editor, but it sounds like a winner to me. When can we shoot the story?"

"We're starting the work this Saturday. Early in the morning. Maybe if you come in the afternoon we'll have made some visible progress ... Also, some of these guys do this stuff for a living and required a little persuading. I kind of hinted that the camera would be good to them. Maybe you could pan over some of the logos on the work trucks? Maybe even an on-site interview? A little free publicity, and those guys'll whistle while they work."

"I see. I'll see what I can do," her voice was receptive, a relief to Frank who cringed at the thought of appearing needy in any way. "So, Saturday around lunchtime?"

"Saturday it is."

"Okay. Goodbye, Mr. Sta— Goodbye, Frank"

As Frank dropped the phone into the charger, Oscar breached the door of The Bull and clicked his cane over to the bar, a bit slower than usual. Nursing a gauze-wrapped hand, he climbed onto a stool and draped himself over the countertop. "Howdy, Frank," he mustered after a long sigh. "How's the wife and kids?"

Frank poured him a beer. "Oscar, my friend. I have news for you."

***

Ms. Hinch was the head therapist of Derek's anger management group, which he was compelled to attend twice a week for three months as a stipulation of his probation. He had already completed one month and had quickly decided there was zero to gain from the woman's inane lectures and group exercises. It was a phenomenal waste of time.

The nine participants sat in a semicircle of multicolored chairs in a meeting room at the Fulton Springs Community Center, trying not to snore as the woman droned on.

"Let's imagine that our partner is running late for dinner after we have spent a long time preparing a meal," said Ms. Hinch, an aging hippie with spectacles and a tantrum of red hair. "Our partner promised they would be home at a certain time, but they're not going to make it. We're irritated. This happens a lot. How should we react?"

She stood before a scowling brick of a man and peered down at her attendance list.

"Mr. Baumhauer," she said, addressing the large man. "How do we typically react when our wife is running late?"

"I'm not married," he muttered.

"Very well, but for the purpose of the exercise let's use a little imagination. What if it were your little brother? Or even a good friend who is late for dinner?"

"I don't know," said Baumhauer.

"Pardon me?" she said.

He raised his voice, "*I don't know how I'd react.*" A judge had ordered Mr. Baumhauer to attend these classes after he shoved his neighbor's head in a mailbox, having found leaves from next door that had blown onto his driveway.

"In such a situation, would you behave calmly?" asked Ms. Hinch.

"Yes," he grumbled.

"Pardon me?"

"Yes, I'd behave calmly, dammit! Now move on to someone

else!"

The idea had occurred to Derek that for a bunch of so-called experts, the people who ran these therapy sessions did not seem to have a firm grasp on their field of study. Their patients allegedly needed to better "manage" their anger, but the therapeutic methods the instructors employed were counterproductive from the outset, practically begging for ridicule and admonishment. Furthermore, the fact that the participants were all forced against their will to attend the classes made them resentful of the very circumstances that compelled their presence—and the therapists were plainly perceived as agents of this injustice. Nothing could make a person angrier than sitting through anger management therapy.

"When faced with such a challenging situation, it is important first and foremost to remain calm. Take a moment to evaluate your situation and respond to your anger. This is different than *reacting* to your anger. *Reaction* is a learned, impulsive behavior. *Responding* allows you to examine various solutions to your situation and choose the best strategy." She always gave a broad, sunny smile to emphasize her point, as though she were talking to a kindergarten class.

Not one attendee was absorbing a word of her lecture because they were too busy focusing their contempt on her ridiculous face, the inescapable squall of her voice, the wall clock that didn't work, or how lousy it was that some authority figure could confiscate their freedom for two afternoons a week and replace it with these asinine group sessions.

"There are many ways to respond to your anger. For example, in stressful situations you can use silly mental pictures to help diffuse your temper. Let's do an exercise with the case of our partner who is running late for dinner. Try using funny mental pictures to accentuate the positive, as we talked about last week. Picture yourself in Wonderland, at the Mad Hatter's Tea Party. Our crazy spouse, Mr. White Rabbit, is running late—*again*—and we're all sitting around and waiting." Ms. Hinch pantomimed the act of looking at her watch, rolling her eyes to feign exasperation and tapping her foot as though waiting. Then she put her hand to her eyes as if shielding the sun and said, "Finally, I see that Crazy Mr. Rabbit coming around the bend."

She assigned Mr. White Rabbit a cartoonish voice, "*'I'm late! I'm late! For a very important date!'*" To illustrate her story, Ms. Hinch hopped like a rabbit across the floor, oblivious to the fact that the nine adults glowering at her viewed this behavior as little more than the bizarre ravings of a madwoman.

"Since he'll be late no matter what, how can we make something positive of the situation?" she asked the room. "How can the Mad Hatter, the Cheshire Cat and Mr. Dormouse make something positive of the situation? You can look at it this way: Your partner's tardiness has awarded you with extra time! With this extra time, you can read a book chapter. You can watch the news. You can file your nails. The idea is to make lemonade out of lemons!" She smiled to punctuate her idea.

"This is bullshit," said Mr. Baumhauer.

Derek agreed. Ms. Hinch was giving him a headache.

***

The ear-ringing racket of rattling jackhammers clashed with the reedy squeal of electric drills. The Stonewall renovation was afoot, with a busy troop of tradesmen milling about the jobsite like a frenzied nest of hornets. A large white van adorned with a "Channel 5 Alive" logo pulled up to the curb, ushering out Daphne Shields and her two-man news crew.

"Looks like a lot of action," said Greg Iris, the videographer, as he raised the camera and hit Record.

As soon as Barry Finkelstein saw the red light of the camera glow to life, he cinched up his T-shirt in a tight knot beneath his breasts and jumped in front of the lens, shaking his ample hips and rolling his white gelatinous gut in an obscene belly dance.

"Put me on TV!" he cooed to the camera, "I'm ready for my 15 seconds!" Barry ran his fingers through his thinning hair like a runway model.

"Barry, act civilized!" said Frank, clapping dust from his hands as he approached. He extended the right one and greeted each journalist with a firm shake, his hand dry and callused.

"Thank you for coming to see us," he said, mostly to Daphne. "What you're looking at is genuine grassroots community activism. Being a good neighbor—that sort of thing. Even Barry, here, is an angel sent from heaven on high." Frank stretched a teasing grin.

Barry, the red-nosed, bespectacled electrician, curtsied and said, "Howdy, welcome to the Manhattan Project," then bounded away to lend his skills where needed.

Daphne's face brightened. "Looks like a colorful cast of characters."

"Yep. Barry was struck by lightning two years ago. Hasn't been the same since … Now, let me show you how we make the sausage." Frank led them to the war zone.

A local news crew on the premises was a Big Deal to the workers, most of whom knew each other from The Bull. As the camera made its rounds, the younger guys rolled up their shirt sleeves and tried to look like they were not flexing. The women fiddled with their eye makeup obsessively. Some of the more familiar volunteers tried to embarrass their friends on camera with ice fights and fat jokes. The camera was downright distracting, and most of the work deteriorated into a party with power tools, but it was serving Frank's purpose well: positive public relations.

"This is the Ortiz family!" shouted Frank over the din of machinery, gesturing the cameraman to three men directing a chute of liquid concrete into wooden forms for the new front steps. "Jorge and his brothers Juan and Paulo—a more conscientious concrete crew you are not apt to find!"

Frank gave them a hearty thumbs-up. The three men waved to the camera and shouted "hola!" in unison.

Next, he kneeled near a red-headed young man who was wearing knee pads and bending over a brick, splitting it with a hammer and cold chisel. "This fella's named Phillip," said Frank, waving a hand before the worker's face, "but everybody calls him Opie. He's a 22-year-old professional mason. Self-employed. Owns his own business. Ain't that right, Ope?"

Opie gave an affirmative salute and returned to his work. Frank hooked his arm for the Channel 5 team to follow. "Opie's deaf," he told Daphne, "but he's never let that slow him down."

Frank led them to rows of work trucks, some with magnetic signs, others with spray-painted stencils on the doors that listed only phone numbers and trade skills: "Drywall + Decks + Trim Carpentry." Greg made sure to get a slow, steady camera pan of the information to appease the volunteers.

"We all care about Mr. Stonewall," explained Frank. "Even my family is here. My son is inside the house repairing the stair rail, and my wife is a metalwork artist; she's contributing a sculpture for Oscar's new front yard. We're not just patching some holes in this place—we're doing our best to make it a place of pride for the city—especially if it's going to be sitting in the front yard of our yet-to-be-built shopping center," Frank smirked.

Daphne instructed Greg and the sound technician to set up a tripod.

"I need to get an establishing shot," she told Frank. "You in the foreground, all the commotion in the background. I'll introduce the segment in a voice-over and transition into you telling us what we're seeing here, framing the story for the viewer. Can you do that for us?"

"Ma'am," said Frank. "I believe I can."

***

As Frank stepped into his living room, a pair of big, brown, bashful eyes peeked out at him from around the hallway corner. He braced himself as his daughter Nora sprang from her hiding place like a flying squirrel. He scooped her up in mid-air and swung her around as she giggled with glee.

"Good evening, beautiful," he said, "and how was your day?"

"It was good, Daddy. I missed you."

"I missed you, too." He buried his face in hers, rubbing noses in an Eskimo kiss.

He delicately lowered her to the floor and shrugged off his leather jacket. The mouth-watering aroma of chicken and biscuits was wafting from the kitchen, where Fancy was preparing dinner. She was still wearing her workshop coveralls, stirring the gravy with a large wooden spoon. Frank encircled her from behind and planted a kiss on the smooth, coffee-colored skin of her neck. Up close he smelled a hint of welded metal still clinging to her clothes from her latest creation.

"Hello, Babe." He whispered in her ear. She turned and kissed him hello as Nora crashed into both of them, hugging them around the thighs.

"How did it go with the television crew?" she said, returning to her sauce.

"Good, I think. They took a lot of footage and did some interviews. I think it'll be a good piece."

"Daddy, are you going to be on TV?" piped Nora, who had plopped down on the floor to wrestle with the dog, a plump, fluffy cocker spaniel named Raleigh.

"I might be on Monday night," he said. "For a minute, anyway."

"Your Daddy did a noble thing today, Nora. He helped a man in need."

"I didn't do much at all," said Frank. "Made some phone calls, that's about it. Everybody pitched in, and we'll be back at it tomorrow. Made some real progress today, though. You ought to see the place. Oscar couldn't believe his eyes, and you should've seen his face when he saw your sculpture." He dipped his finger into the gravy, and slurped off the goodness.

"You got the ball rolling, Frank. Don't say you didn't. And that's why the people around here look up to you. You get things done."

Frank ate heartily that night, scarfing down some homemade fried chicken, green beans, mashed potatoes and buttermilk biscuits with sawmill gravy. He slept at ease with a full stomach, a supportive family and a momentary feeling of contentment.

***

Just hours before Monday's "Community Heartbeat" aired on Channel 5, the gavel fell in the city council chambers, granting Mayor Cornelius and his council members a 30-percent salary increase—ostensibly to cover "cost of living expenses." The previous year had also come with a 30-percent increase to cover the cost of living. The year before that, the mayor and councilmen had enjoyed a 25-percent increase for the same reason, and this all went unnoticed by most of the people of Fulton Springs.

Frank told Fancy he was amazed everyone else in town hadn't gone tits up because living was becoming cost-prohibitive.

***

"Shut your mouths, everybody, it's coming on TV!" shouted the Napoleonic Frieda Collins from her saddle at the slot machine. An obedient hush fell over the crowd at The Bull. Though only five feet tall and elderly, nobody messed with Frieda. She and her friend Betsy turned around on their stools for a better line of sight.

"Good evening, this is Daphne Shields with 'Community Heartbeat' on location in Fulton Springs with a volunteer project to renovate the home of Oscar Stonewall." On The Bull's television screen was a wide-angle

shot of the property, the scene full of clanging construction noise with laborers milling about dutifully.

"Stonewall, an 84-year old disabled veteran and longtime Fulton Springs resident, was issued an eviction notice because his house was deemed by the city to be unfit for habitation."

Oscar appeared in a camera close-up. *"They ain't never even been inside my house. This is just more bullcrap from that jackass mayor,"* he said.

Cut back to Daphne Shields at the work site: *"When word got out that Stonewall was losing his home, his friends and neighbors stepped in to help—and did so in a big way—all organized by a familiar face in Alabama, racing legend turned barbecue owner, Frank 'the Bull' Standish."*

Close-up on Frank, exterior shot in front yard of Stonewall property: *"We just couldn't let this stand. It's our local government out of control—again—and we weren't going to let a friend lose his home. While Oscar's home wasn't pretty, it was structurally sound. He was singled out because the mayor wants his property for the new mall. If we let the government take his property, then whose house are they going to take next? Oscar was here long before Cornelius was elected mayor, and we're going to make sure this is where he stays."* On hearing this, the patrons of the Bull erupted in a cacophony of hoots and hollers, sending beer soaring into the air from the clashing of glasses in exuberant toasts.

Back to Daphne, the camera following her around the work area to document the progress: *"Local businessmen in the construction field graciously donated time, materials—and a lot of perspiration—to completely remodel the Stonewall property, featuring a new paint job, reconstructed steps and sidewalk, roof and window repair and even fresh landscaping. Channel 5 met some of the friendly volunteers, including Ortiz and Sons Concrete, Caldwell Masonry, Butler Heating & Air, Warner Plumbing and Finkelstein Electrical. We experienced a genuine sense of family from this tight-knit community."* The bar went wild for the TV exposure. Daphne's editor was careful to insert a shot of the work trucks, showing all the logos and phone numbers

A medium shot of Selby, his face smudged and pipe wrench in hand: *"Oscar's too old to handle this kind of work, so of course we'll pitch in. The people you see here are the salt of the earth. Besides, our mayor's a bum!"*

Back to Daphne, standing in front of the completed home, a stark and handsome improvement on all fronts. *"By Sunday evening, this local crew of weekend remodelers had completely turned the house around, addressing every aspect of the city's complaint, beautifying the exterior and even adding a couple of surprises to commemorate the occasion."* The camera closed in on the new centerpiece of Oscar's front yard—a 5-foot copper sculpture of a bucking bull, skillfully shaped and soldered with artistic precision by the hands of Fancy Standish.

The news segment closed with Oscar, his creased face glistening with tears in a tight frame. *"I can't believe it,"* he sniffed. *"I'm so blessed to have friends, to have neighbors like this. I can't thank them enough."*

The women in The Bull let out a collective, *"Awwwwwww..."*

The segment was a hit.

***

"Goooooooood morning, Birmingham!" boomed the stereo in Frank's pickup truck. "You're tuned in to the million-mile-an-hour Mouth of the South, 'Madman' Marty Madigan and his band of merry men, bringing you all the latest and greatest news commentary at the local and national level—but today we're focusing on a local story, a

heartwarming story, don't you think so, Vanessa?"

"It is a nice story," said Vanessa from the producer's desk in a soft, singsong voice nurtured for radio broadcasting. "Inspiring, even. We need more stories like this on the Marty Madigan Show."

"Yes we do. We certainly do. Well, listeners, if you happened to tune into Channel 5 News last night you may have caught the station's 'Community Heartbeat' segment in which a group of concerned and caring citizens joined forces to remodel a neighbor's home in order to fight a notice of eviction from the city of Fulton Springs, based on the grounds that the property was deemed 'a blight to the community.' We've tracked down the homeowner and are happy to have him with us on the show via telephone this morning to shine some light on what happened. Oscar Stonewall, welcome to the Marty Madigan show."

Frank had received an early morning phone call with advanced word of Oscar's interview.

"Thank you for having me," said Oscar over the air, static popping in the reception.

"Oscar, how long have you been living in your home?"

Slowly he responded, "Forty years. I own the house outright and I've been living in that same spot for decades before that jackass Mayor Cornelius ever took office, telling people where to live and how to live."

"Why did the city officials consider your home to be a 'blight?'"

"My house is and was solid as a rock. Maybe a little behind the times, but I'm too old to keep up with the 'Joneses' and all the new bells and whistles. And I live off a fixed pension, so I ain't got a whole lot of spending money. But that's beside the point, really. The real reason they wanted me out of the house is because of where that house is sitting. They've been trying to buy me out for the last eight months, and I keep telling 'em to go jump in a lake. They're wanting to expand a shopping mall right over my doorstep, but I told 'em time and time again that I ain't movin'. So they figured they'd get tough and kick me out. But they didn't count on The Bull."

"What's The Bull?"

"The Bull is a barbecue joint over on Main Street in Fulton Springs where I spend some time. But it's a lot more than just a place. It's like a family. It's a community, and they pitched in to fix up my old house so I could stay put."

"As I understand it, your friends and neighbors actually gave up their free time and even donated building materials to remodel your house and stop the eviction."

"Yeah, that's about the long and short of it," Oscar laughed. "And I couldn't be more grateful, even though I suspect that those folks had an inkling of an ulterior motive."

"And what would that motive be?"

"Oh, to tick off the mayor, of course," Oscar laughed again, hoarsely, and coughed to clear his throat. "See, Fulton Springs is kind of divided between people like us at The Bull who just want to be left alone, and Mayor Cornelius and his folks, who want to dictate to everyone else how to live their lives."

"What do you mean by that? Aside from the eviction, what has the mayor done to control your life?"

"Starts with taxes, taxes, taxes!" shouted Oscar, growing further impassioned. "I have never seen such a steep increase in taxes in all my life as I have since Cornelius took the mayor's chair. When people have less money in their wallets because of higher taxes, they have less money to spend on their own lives, whether that's feeding their kids or taking a vacation."

"What else you got? High taxes is a tired complaint, and everyone makes it every election year. Besides, that revenue is then reinvested into Fulton Springs, is it not?"

"I haven't seen much reinvestment. Somebody needs to look into the books, 'cause somethin' smells fishy. Mayor supposedly raised a boat-load of money for new school computers, but word has it that the computers never showed up. And our property taxes are jumping seems like every year, which probably goes to the mayor's raises. The mayor and city council have been raising their own pay each and every year, so I guess the councilmen are getting 'reinvested in,' but everybody else in town gets the shaft. This year a new city tax was added to our gas bill!

"And that ain't all. He tries to tell you where and when you can have a beer, and I don't like being told what I can and can't do. He tells you when and where you can smoke with all the new laws he passes. If he can muster it—and one day he probably will—he'll outlaw drinking and smoking altogether, just like he's trying to do with gambling right now."

"There's gambling in Fulton Springs?"

"The Bull's got two bingo machines. Slot machines. Nobody even uses 'em except a couple of old ladies, but Cornelius is declaring war on that Great Evil. Gotta stop those blue-hairs from spending their loose change, you know?"

Frank, listening to the interview on the radio of his pickup truck, slapped his forehead. He was hoping the slot machines had drifted off the mayor's radar screen, but he was bound to hear about this.

"See, the mayor says gambling is sinful, so it's gotta be stopped," continued Oscar. "I say restricting the freedoms of grown, honest, tax-paying adults is sinful, but I ain't a preacher so what do I

45

know, right?"

"Well, you obviously have a beef with the mayor—"

"We all have a fight with that jackass. Hell, he just used the power of his office to try to kick me outta my home in favor of a private business that he has financial ties to. To me, that's fascism. It's what I fought against in the war."

"If he's so terrible, then why don't the people of Fulton Springs just vote him out of office?"

"We'd be willing to try," said Oscar, "but ain't nobody even run against him in the last two election cycles. And he's got all the support of the First Baptist Church."

"The First Baptist Church of Fulton Springs?" asked Madigan. "Isn't that the one that broadcasts its Sunday morning service on television?"

"That's the one. They all vote for the mayor 'cause they know they'll be taken care of. They're comfortable, so they don't have to think too hard about things. See, Cornelius used to be the preacher there and stepped down to run for mayor. But everybody knows good and well that he stills calls the shots. And, the city of Fulton Springs just signed over a huge parcel of land, sold for pennies on the dollar, to the church so it can expand its compound even further. That place is like a cult, I swear. But as long as the mayor keeps granting the church those sweetheart deals, and granting its members all the city contracts, he can count on their votes—and that's a helluva lot of votes."

"Sounds fishy to me …"

"Fishy, hell. *It stinks to high heaven!* But that's the reality. This time we won, though. The Bull came through in the end, and the city can't evict me. I guess they'll have to build that shopping mall right next to me, instead of on top of me. We'll be neighbors."

"Well, congratulations on keeping your home, Mr. Stonewall. It sounds like the people of Fulton Springs have some things to work out with their city government. I hope you'll keep us up-to-date on any further developments."

"I'd be happy to," said Oscar.

"It was nice to speak with you, Mr. Stonewall, and thanks for joining us on The Marty Madigan—"

"—Wait, I got one more thing to say to the people of Fulton Springs."

"Okay, go right ahead."

"Vote Frank Standish for mayor!" and with a soft click the line was disconnected. Frank's cigarette fell from his lips. He frantically hopped around the seat slapping at the coal to avoid a burn on the upholstery.

"There you have it, ladies and gentlemen. Sounds like Mr. Stonewall already has a new mayoral candidate in mind. As is our policy here at the station, we welcome Mayor Cornelius of Fulton Springs to call the show and provide his side of the story. But right now we're up against a hard break, so stay tuned for more hard-hitting news/talk right here on WROC 107.7."

Frank lit two new cigarettes. The shouted chorus of the Beastie Boys' "No Sleep 'til Brooklyn" rose in volume as bumper music before the commercial. He cranked the radio back over to the country/western station and steered to work.

***

Mayor Cornelius slammed a bulbous fist on the table. "*What the HELL is HAPPENING around here!"*

Pierce Mathers turned off the radio and shook his head in consolation.

"Like a bolt from the blue I'm getting roasted on both TV and radio? By my constituents! They've got us looking like a bunch of monsters, kicking the elderly out of their homes."

"But that's pretty much what we were doing."

"Don't be a wise-ass, son. You know as well as I do that what matters is *perception!* And we are now being perceived negatively." The mayor blotted his forehead with a handkerchief. "We've got to keep the appearance of moral integrity if we're going to keep the church in the ballot box. We need those votes for me to stay mayor — that's my ass, *and yours!* Being portrayed like we're corrupt and un-Christian ... that could blow up in our faces. We've got to stop it."

"You know where it started," said Mathers.

The mayor stood from his chair and walked to his office window, gazing toward the other end of Main Street. "Of course I do," he said. "Standish."

"Mr. Stonewall was encouraging people to vote for him in the next election."

"Yes, I heard that, Piercey." Raindrops speckled the window glass, distorting the view of the cars and trucks that circulated through the town square. Cornelius saw the town as his kingdom and was unaccustomed to having his authority questioned publicly. It was wounding. "Is Standish running?"

"I haven't heard that officially," said Mathers. "But I suppose he could have that trick up his sleeve. He's kind of a local hero with his racing history and his bar. If he threw his hat in the race, he could pose a problem."

Cornelius licked his tongue around the rim of his Styrofoam cup to suck off the last drops of stale coffee. "Could pose a problem," he repeated ethereally. "What to do?" He was speaking to himself as if in a ghostly trance. He was entertaining dreamily irrational ways to eliminate his problem—by means of fire, knife, bullet or bomb.

"Nip it," said Mathers.

The mayor surfaced from his daze. "What?"

"That's what we've got to do. Ever watch 'The Andy Griffith Show'? It's the wisdom of Barney Fife: The minute it looks like there's gonna be trouble, you got to nip it. Nip it in the bud."

"Nip it?" said Cornelius.

Pierce nodded. "In the bud."

The mayor nodded slowly. Mathers was right, of course. It would be unwise to allow Standish to gain further momentum in the arena of public opinion if he were planning a run for office. They needed to hit back, and hit hard. The Mayor peered up at Mathers from a dark brood and said, "So how do you propose we nip it?"

***

Frank was not surprised by the arrival of the Fulton Springs police officers, but he winced at the sight of Officer Art Brookings, a personal friend and longtime patron. There were four officers, and Art hung toward the rear of the pack, literally hanging his head in shame.

"Is there a problem, fellas?" Frank asked with a cigarette dangling from the corner of his mouth. He push-broomed a pile of dirt to the corner of the room and leaned the broom's long, wooden handle against the wall, wiping his hands on his apron. It was well after the lunchtime rush, and only a few customers remained.

"We're here with a warrant," said a tall, heavy officer with wavy black hair and a moustache. His name tag said *Farling*. Frank knew him as the shot-caller among the local cops, and had never liked him. "We're confiscating your electronic slot machines. They're illegal in Fulton Springs, and you are unlawfully engaging in organized gambling on these premises."

Art forced a half smile at Frank, turning his palms to the air. "*Sorry*," he mouthed in a silent plea.

Frank nodded to Art.

Frank had two machines in the corner of the bar. One was currently occupied by Frieda Collins, the 77-year old widow who tried her luck at the 25-cent coin-op machines a few times a week. Frank had actually installed the machines at the request of Frieda and her longtime friend Betsy Willingham, both regular patrons of the restaurant who felt they had grown too old to keep traveling over state lines to hit the Mississippi casinos. The machines at The Bull were among Frieda and Betsy's select joys in life.

Frieda, overhearing the discussion, looked over her shoulder at the officers and said plainly, "I ain't going anywhere."

The officers looked at one another, then turned to Frank inquisitively.

Frank shrugged. "Don't look at me. You want the machines; she's your problem." He backed away. It was well known around The Bull that when crossed, little old Frieda Collins could morph from a sweet and dainty grandmotherly figure to a frothing, snarling fire-bomb of female fury. She was a human bear trap with beehive hair.

Officer Farling advanced across the room.

"Ma'am, I'm afraid I'm going to have to ask you to step away from the machine."

Frieda ignored him as though he were a light breeze.

"Ma'am," he said louder. "You need to realize that if you refuse to leave, then you are interfering with an official police matter."

Frieda pulled the handle of the slot machine, completely unfazed. It rolled out three stars and two hearts. She pulled the handle again, seemingly oblivious to his presence.

The officer forced a cough. "Excuse me, *ma'am!*"

"Don't you raise your voice at me!" she warned. "I'm not harming anybody by using this machine. So, you'd just better leave me alone."

Farling grew agitated. "Ma'am, time to go," he said firmly, but she had turned her attention back to the game.

To encourage her compliance, he placed his hand lightly on Frieda's shoulder. It was a dire mistake.

Like a pouncing puma, Frieda whirled on her stool and clobbered Farling over the head with her overstuffed purse. He cried out, and Frieda screeched like a mad bat. She swung the purse upward in an arc, smashing Farling under the chin.

The whole scene exploded into a ridiculous wrestling match as the other officers—all except Brookings—struggled to subdue the thrashing woman and force her into the back of a patrol car. Frieda assaulted the cops with a barrage of profanities so blue they seemed incongruous with her age; she even derided the size of the officers' manhood and the honor of their mothers. By the time she was locked in the back of a black-and-white, she held two handfuls of hair, and Officer Farling had a bloody face and two new bald spots.

The patrol car disappeared down Main in the direction of the city jail, with Frieda locked in the back, just as the freight truck backed into the parking lot to carry away The Bull's two offending machines.

Frank was slapped with a citation for the slot machines and a second citation for smoking in a prohibited area. The sum total was $1,500, payable to the City of Fulton Springs.

***

"They're dying for him to run," Derek said to Fancy as he rifled through the refrigerator for the makings of a sandwich. "People are talking about organizing a campaign and everything."

Fancy was putting away dishes from the washer. "As far as I know, nobody has even asked him if he's interested."

"But you do think he'd be interested, right? I mean, with as much crap as he's been putting up with from the city?"

"Well, I know he thinks that *someone* should be interested. Is that someone him?" She smiled as she organized the silverware drawer. "I do believe he would do a good job, I'll give you that."

"Down at the bar they're talking like it's a foregone conclusion. I think he may be running whether he likes it or not."

"Where's Daddy going to run?" Nora asked from the kitchen table, without looking up from her intensive coloring of a blue dog on a red planet.

"Run for mayor," said Derek.

Nora looked up. "Pop for mayor?"

"Mayor Pop," said Derek. "Mayor Frank Standish ... sounds better than Mayor Jackass."

"Son, please watch your mouth around Nora."

"Yeah, jackass!" chided Nora.

Fancy always called Derek "Son," but he never capitulated and called her "Mom." There was no animosity involved; rather, he extended her every other grace and courtesy that he had granted his own mother, who passed away suddenly of a brain aneurism when he was thirteen. "Mom" was a word he reserved especially for her, Cynthia Standish, formerly Cynthia Hamilton. Derek and his mother had been very close, more so than he and his father, whom he greatly admired but often felt awkward and humbled in his shadow.

His father was a local racing legend, while Derek had been uncoordinated in sports and socially awkward in high school. While females swooned over his father, Derek was dumbstruck by girls and never knew how to talk to them. He was interested in skateboarding and punk rock music while utterly bored by class elections, holiday dances or the celebrated football team of Fulton Springs High School. He loved his dad dearly but felt that he and Frank were stuck at opposite ends of the social spectrum, and Derek had no idea how to fix it.

As almost any teen reeling from such a tragedy would have behaved, Derek was at first resistant to his father and Fancy's courtship. Although it began three years after his mother's death, anytime was too soon to Derek. There were times when he spewed forth some dreadfully foul invective toward Fancy, once even dropping the mother of all insults to a black woman—the N-word. That ugly racial sentiment did not genuinely exist in Derek's heart, but at the time he felt betrayed by his dad, yet found it easier to project all his vinegar onto Fancy. He could not stand the sight of the woman; her great transgression being her mere existence as a love interest to his father. That night they had been in a heated argument, and Derek had nearly exhausted his bank of profanity. He grasped for any weapon that could inflict pain, and that powerful word was hidden deep in the darkest shadows of his arsenal. He found it, and the pain came in spades—hers and his. He realized the stabbing wound he had delivered as soon as that acrid word left his lips. "Nigger!"

She reflected its sting with a wordless wilting of her eyes. Her brow had quivered, her shoulders sank, and tears welled. She retreated from the room, closing the door behind her with a hollow thump. She left with silent dignity. An elegant response.

Frank had witnessed the exchange but reacted only with a quiet, rueful stare. Nothing needed to be said. Derek knew that in Frank's world view, such an insult deserved an old-fashioned ass whooping. They both knew he was asking for it. But no punishment could have dealt a lashing like the revolting self-disgust Derek felt for having sunk to such mindless, petulant depths. He instantly felt shame as never before, and his father was counting on it. Frank spat on Derek's bedroom floor before walking away to let the guilt gnaw his son in silence. Derek sat on his bed for hours, agonizing over his actions. It was an effective form of punishment.

It was also the rock-bottom moment of his and his stepmother's contentious relationship. Afterward, Derek's deep sense of remorse made him so hypersensitive to Fancy's well-being that he showered her with all manner of kindness and good regard. Over time, they grew close, the guilt waned and gave way to true mutual respect, and for all practical purposes he had gained a new mother and dear friend, and eventually an adorable new sibling. Born a year after Frank and Fancy were married, Nora was a sweet and sassy little sister who was cuter than the dimples on a baby's butt.

But Derek always insisted on calling Fancy by her name; there was still only one "Mom."

"Pop is just what the city needs," continued Derek. "The problem with public servants today is they want a career out of the job. They compromise their values to keep themselves in power. Pop doesn't want a career. He'd just focus on fixing what's broke and then go back to work at The Bull. Get in, get out, no foolin' about." Derek spread a thick layer of mayonnaise over his slice of bread. He was building a double-decker ham and cheddar on rye. "That's the kind of man the city needs. Someone invested in the city, not in a city career. Do the job, then let the next person go to bat, keeping the people in positions of power honest and focused on the needs of the electorate, and not the needs of their next election." He tore a big bite from his sandwich.

"I like it," said Fancy. "'Get in, get out, no fooling about.' Sounds like a campaign slogan."

***

Frank walked through the door of The Bull and felt a distinctive electricity in the air. He had somehow sensed it even from the parking lot, and found the restaurant abuzz with activity on his behalf. The campaign machine was up and running with people bustling about the place excitedly and phoning their friends to ask for their vote—all this despite the fact that Frank had not even committed his candidacy.

Sharon McClendon was taping fliers all over the bar. Frank pulled one from the wall. "Frank Standish Will Stand for the People" it stated in red and blue lettering. At the bottom was a photo of Frank in his younger years, hanging out the window of an old race car and waving to fans. He remembered that race fondly—at Red Mountain Motor Speedway, his second win of the circuit, which he accomplished by mere inches.

Derek, Selby and Oscar were hunkered over one of the dining tables, diligently sketching Xs and Os on a notepad as if designing a football play. Accompanying them was Nathan Stevenson, the Fulton Springs parks and recreation officer, a bar regular who greeted Frank with a broad smile and an eager handshake.

"Frank, it's good to see you," he said, pumping Frank's hand vigorously. "I'm so glad you decided to run. I was hoping somebody would throw their hat in the ring. I want you to know that you've got my full support. I'm know I'm considered an 'insider' since I work for the city and all, but I assure you that my loyalty does not lie with Mayor Cornelius, particularly with his idiotic idea to prohibit fishing along Six Mile Creek."

"Prohibit fishing?" said Frank.

"Exactly! Prohibit fishing! Of all the silly things!" said Stevenson, miming the action of casting a rod. He was a high-strung and very expressive man, and when he spoke it seemed his hands were in constant motion, pantomiming his point with charades. "But the mayor got rattled when he heard you were running—that's the word around city hall, anyway. So he's building a war chest, planning on out-spending you and basically drowning out the opposing message with PR and advertisements, that sort of thing."

"What's that got to do with fishing?"

"It's got to do with money," said Stevenson as he traced the shape of a dollar sign in the air with his finger. "He just sucked up a huge campaign contribution from an organization called Free the Fish. It's kind of like 'Save the Whales' I guess, but they target fresh-water streams and lakes that are used for recreational fishing, claiming they're defending the rights of the fish and all. Particularly, for something called the yellow-bellied spunk minnow."

"Yellow-bellied what?"

"Spunk minnow. See, the way it works is, this group contributes to political campaigns with the understanding that when elected, the officials in question will reciprocate with certain favors … in this case, prohibiting recreational fishing on public waterways."

"I grew up fishing Six Mile," said Frank.

"So did I," said Derek.

"We all did," chimed Oscar.

Frank and his father used to spend long afternoons canoeing the Six Mile, angling for crappie and catfish. When Derek was old enough, Frank continued the tradition with his son. Six Mile Creek was a special place in Fulton Springs, a natural retreat rich with wildlife and deep with memories. Now it would be subjected to new government regulations.

"It's all about money," said Stevenson, shrugging his shoulders. "I'm the parks and recreation officer, and the mayor is taking the *recreation* out of the parks. Nuts to him!" He punched the palm of his hand.

Frank re-taped Sharon's homespun campaign flier to the wall. He took a deep breath and said, "Look, guys, I appreciate the enthusiasm, but I don't have any kind of 'war chest.' And I don't know much about politics."

For a moment everyone stood in silence staring at Frank. They did not seem to accept what he had said and waited for something else.

"We know you're not a politician, Frank," said Oscar. "That's why we want you in office."

Frank looked them over, one by one, and realized that if he

did not run for office, then no one else would. He would be stuck with Cornelius again. With that dark cloud on the horizon, he could not muster a protest to their call to action. He felt as though he were caught in one of the tractor beams he had seen on Star Trek, a gravity ray that grabs other spaceships and slowly retrieves them into the cargo bay. Resistance was futile.

The crowd took his silence as tacit approval of the whole affair. Frank Standish would run for mayor of Fulton Springs, whether he liked it or not.

***

The Bull flourished into full-blown Standish campaign headquarters within a matter of hours. The regulars of the bar, unvarying in their support for Frank's election bid, had each assumed their roles organically as though instinctively spreading their wings for flight, the most natural act in the world. There was a "crafts corner," where posters were being made, as well as a "telecommunications center," consisting of three chairs around a table where Sharon McClendon and two friends were coordinating support calls to local friends and family from their cell phones. Derek was punching on a laptop keyboard, initiating development of his father's official campaign website. Selby and Nathan Stevenson had been dispatched to city hall to get the nitty-gritty on all the legal red tape required to run for election in Fulton Springs.

Frank had never put much thought into how a public servant should conduct himself, but he reasoned that the most fundamental approach would be to determine the concerns of the people he would be representing. So, Frank bellied up to a table with a tall glass of sweet tea for a back-and-forth with anyone who wanted to speak to him about the trajectory of the city. And word spread quickly.

"An open bidding process for contract jobs in Fulton Springs," said Buck Butler. He lifted his shades over his forehead and rested them on top of the red bandana wrapping his scalp. "I ain't asking for any favors, just a level playing field. Bobby and I have the most respectable HVAC business in town, but we got completely shut out of the contracts for the new mall because they all went to Hayworth HVAC. The new mall is a package deal that the city set up with the developer. The construction of the mall is being partially subsidized by the city as an incentive for the new businesses. Herbert Hayworth is a deacon at the Big Church with Cornelius and the other council members. That's why he got the contract—a total backroom, 'good ol' boy' deal. The fact is, we could've easily underbid Hayworth. And when you're talking about publicly subsidized contracts, it's not just the competing contractors who are getting screwed over by a no-bid process. No matter how you stretch it, the taxpayer gets the short end when they've gotta foot that outlandish bill from Hayworth—and for sub-par work, I might add."

Frank was intently taking notes on a legal pad as he interviewed The Bull's regulars, one by one, about concerns they had with the local government. He soon filled up 15 pages of notes, and this was the first night of his "man on the street" research.

"Aw, shoot, what do I know, Frank?" asked Barry Finkelstein, wiggling his bulbous rump into the chair across from Frank. "I guess I can't complain. I'm happy as a pea in a pod ..." he trailed off and his eyes rolled backward as if searching for something in the back of his brain.

"—Wait, I do want the pothole fixed," he continued, one of his eyebrows cocked up suspiciously. "There's five houses on my street, and we all gotta drive over this pothole to go anywhere. Been there for years, a big sucker at least eight inches deep. It's hell on your tires. I wrote to the mayor about six or seven times, but ain't nothing ever been done. One day I decided to fill it with gravel. That cop Farling caught me doing it and gave me a ticket. For fixing the road!" said Barry. "But every time the fancy-pants folks over in the Brookcrest subdivision get so much as a hairline crack, the city patches it right up." Barry's eyes widened and wobbled in their sockets as if they might fall out of his face. He stood on his chair and raised his fist in the air. "You know, Frankie, when it comes to that mayor, I smell a rat. *A Dirty Rat!*" he screamed.

Frank jotted the complaint in his notepad while separately considering that Barry may be clinically insane.

"I want my slots back!" said Frieda Collins. "Those sonsabitches took my machine and then man-handled me! I think I'm going to sue the city, you know. I swear, that Farling bastard better steer clear of me on the street or I'll run him right down in my Caddy, badge and all! If my husband was still alive he'd have that cop sunk in the Six Mile wearing cement shoes!"

Frank jotted this down, along with a side note to never, ever upset Frieda. News of Frank's call for complaints quickly spread beyond The Bull.

"You aren't the only person who got irritated with me," said the waiter from The Magnolia, whose name turned out to be Evan Pointer, co-owner of the restaurant. "Lots of customers have complained about the smoking ban. When we scouted this location, the smoking laws weren't on the books. As soon as we opened the doors—*BAM!*—we got issued new rules. It's hard to build a clientele when the city's laws are making your customers unhappy with your business."

As Frank peered up from his notes, he saw a growing line of people snaking through the bar and out to the sidewalk, all eager to air their grievances.

***

"Another helpful emotional technique is forgiveness," offered Ms. Hinch through a beaming mouth of yellow teeth during Derek's Thursday session of anger management therapy. *"For those of you with religious inclinations, forgiveness is a very Christian principle. But religious or not, forgiveness remains a very powerful and effective emotional tool for managing our anger."*

Derek checked the time and rubbed his eyes.

"If you are angry, then it's usually because someone or something set you off," said Hinch. *"However, we all make mistakes. Always remember that... I make them. You make them. That's why you're in this class. You made a mistake."*

I was forced into this class by threat of incarceration, thought Derek.

"Reflect on what it means to make a mistake," she said. *"Put yourself in the shoes of the person who has made the mistake, and you'll find it much easier to forgive them. Once you realize the power that comes with forgiveness, you'll find yourself able to handle stressful situations much more easily."*

Derek thought about the litany of circumstances that had landed him in the therapy session. It was unfortunate how friendships could sour over time. He and Pierce Mathers had been friends in elementary school. In Ms. Jacobson's third-grade class they were science fair partners who worked together on a project where they demonstrated the capillary action of a plant using celery and food coloring. In sixth grade they joined the community league football team. Pierce was more physically coordinated, and an early growth spurt gave him more weight and athletic ability than Derek. Derek was built like a cornstalk—all arms and legs, knees and elbows, with no meat on his frame. He was comically awkward on the field and got thrown around like a dog's chew toy. Pierce was a rising star by junior high, and their friendship had faded ever since. Pierce aligned himself with the athletic crowd. Derek stuck with his interests in comic books and horror films.

Although Derek and Pierce once traded baseball cards and action figures, as they entered high school their relationship deteriorated to the point of tyranny. Pierce's new best friend was the cube-shaped, slow-witted nose guard for life, Billy Farling. Derek, who was still skinny, clumsy and—according to Mathers and Farling—weirder by the day, took a lot of abuse as a teenager. His heavy-metal T-shirts and spiky hair didn't help Derek blend into the football fans, and as with any small town in America, whatever sticks up often gets hammered back down.

Throughout high school, Derek endured endless minor assaults, like upturned books in the hallway, frog punches to the shoulder and the constant threat of gym class wedgies. But he also suffered the occasional Special Event, which left extra scar tissue, like the time he was drenched by a urine-filled balloon thrown from a passing school bus. During these Special Events, Mathers, Farling and their traveling circus of popular pimple-faces would orchestrate some especially cruel and humiliating attack in a very public place.

One day, at the end of tenth-grade gym class, Derek was in a locker room stall changing back into his classroom clothes. He had long ago learned to seek refuge in a bathroom stall, because changing in the open area of the locker bay was to invite an endless flood of towel whips, red bellies and other such grab-assery from the athletes. The bigger, more popular kids seemed compelled to demean the weaker ones.

There were six stalls in the locker room, and Derek found five of them occupied by the other typical gym-class victims. The sixth stall was a measure of last resort because it was missing the small metal bar that bolted the door. Making the situation more precarious was the absence of Coach Baker, who generally administered some degree of order during dress-out. The substitute gym teacher was useless, a naïve and inattentive older man who served as little more than a nose-picking background prop to the cast of unruly adolescents. Although Derek recognized the inherent danger of the sixth stall, he had little choice because the period bell would soon ring and he would have to dash across campus for a math quiz. Derek resolved to brave the unlocked stall and had regretted it ever since.

As soon as he unlooped his jockey shorts from his ankle, the door exploded open and six cackling boys lunged at him, wrenching him from the stall, kicking and screaming. They hoisted his flailing nude body above them as if he had just made the winning play of a big game, or as if he were about to be cast into the pits of hell as a sacrificial virgin. The throng of marauders rioted toward the girl's gym across the hallway. They kicked open the double doors and shoved Derek stark naked into the basketball court. The court was divided by three volleyball nets, with three games in progress.

The doors slammed closed behind Derek. He spun to see the shocked faces of his female peers. Time stopped. For a long moment he heard only silence. He felt a draft from the commercial air vents cool his exposed buttocks. A girl's scream broke the silence.

Derek slammed into the doors with his shoulder. They barely budged. Through the narrow windows of the doors he was staring into the contorted faces of Mathers and Farling. They were pressed against the glass, barring his escape, whooping and pointing at his exposed body.

The gym behind him had erupted with the shrill sound of laughter and dehumanizing catcalls. Derek could not face them. He dropped to his knees and buried his face against the closed doors. Tears ran from his eyes. His body was shaking and he began to hyperventilate.

He glanced to the corner of the adjacent wall and spied another exit. He rose to his feet, cupping his private parts. He trotted down the side of the gym, wearing the eyes of 46 young female classmates. His tail-tucked scurry to the door struck the girls as irresistibly hysterical. Their laughter rose with renewed vigor. Crouching to conceal his nether regions hindered his flight, so he abandoned all efforts at modesty and broke into a full-stride nude sprint down the chamber of leers and jeers and cacophonous hysteria, until he finally escaped through the corner door.

He would hear echoes of those laughing young women for the rest of his life.

"To err is human; to forgive divine," said Ms. Hinch, smiling broadly. *"That's a quote from a man named Alexander Pope. He understood the power of forgiveness."*

The gym class episode had taken a heavy toll on Derek. He refused to return to school the rest of the week. He knew that a naked classmate streaking the girls' gym would be hot fodder for the high school rumor mill, and he absolutely refused to put himself on the spicket for a pig roast. His parents never said a word in protest.

"I'm sorry, son." Frank told him on the night of the incident. "Kids should never bully other kids. It's a lousy thing to do."

Derek was sullen, sitting darkly on his bed and losing himself in a handheld video game.

"But that's the way life is, sometimes," said Frank. "It's a load of crap. It is. But I want you to know that I'm here for you. Whatever you need, son." Frank gave him a firm pat on the shoulder and turned to leave.

His invitation struck Derek as odd. I'm here for you? He knew his father as emotionally distant and poorly communicative. It was out of character.

"Did anyone ever bully you?" asked Derek before his dad got to the door.

Frank paused and nodded. "Sure. I think everybody goes through that."

Derek knew his father loved him unconditionally but also knew that his father had trouble identifying with him. Frank could not understand his son's fascination with comic books, superheroes or role-playing games—"egghead stuff" as he called it, which he considered too childish for a teenager. And Frank considered Derek's taste in music to be little more than a fondness for noisy, bizarre stuff that "sounds like a maniac screaming over a car wreck." His dad blamed his oddball interests for enticing the abuse he was getting from his peers, so Derek was intrigued to learn that they finally shared something in common—at some point his dad was enough of an outsider to collect himself a bully.

"When I was young there was a kid named Cyrus Hemphill. Mean kid. He grew up to be a mean adult, too, from what I hear. I guess he didn't like himself any more than anyone else did, because he eventually drank himself to death."

"Did you ever get into a fight with him?"

Frank looked into space, recalling decades. "He roughed me up a good bit. Back then I liked to ride my bicycle around the block. Well, Cyrus considered the street outside his house to be his territory. He didn't much like me riding by. He'd throw rocks and stuff. One time he hit me with a tree branch. Sometimes I'd go home with a busted lip or a black eye."

Derek had stopped playing his game, giving his dad his full attention. "So what'd you do?"

"I kept riding my bike around that block," said Frank. "I was a growing boy. Sure, he was bigger and meaner, but that wasn't always going to be the case. Then, one day your grandmother asked me to borrow a cup of sugar from the Petersons, who lived up the road. On my way back home, I got nailed with a brick that seemed to come right out of thin air. It knocked me completely off my bike. It cut my head, and the plastic cup of sugar went all over the damned place. And the wheel of my bike was warped. Ruined! That's when I heard Cyrus Hemphill laughing his head off. And I kind of snapped. I marched right over to that jackass—right in his front yard, where I had never before had the courage to go. And I beat the ever-loving snot out of that kid. I didn't stop hitting him until his mother ran out of the house and pulled me off him."

"Seriously?" Derek's eyes were as wide as silver dollars.

Frank let out a long whistle and nodded. "Yes, sir. I surprised myself that day. I gave him a black eye and a busted lip. He never bothered me again. And even though I had to walk home with a broken bike that day, I never felt prouder in my life."

"For kicking his butt?"

Frank thought for a moment. "No. For standing up for myself."

The conversation had been a turning point for Derek.

"Here's another one of my favorites," smiled Ms. Hinch to her captives, *"'To forgive is to set a prisoner free and discover that the prisoner was you.'"*

Derek checked the time again. What a bunch of insipid garbage.

"Don't get me wrong. Fighting is not a good thing," Frank had told him, "but a man has to stand his ground. It's my belief that everybody ought to leave each other alone. Live and let live—that's my philosophy. But not everybody shares it. Somebody else always seems to break that rule. Some folks won't live and let live, and instead they seem compelled to give a fella a hard time.

"You've got to be patient when that happens. Don't fly off the handle like an idiot. The Lord says in the Bible that we should turn the other cheek when someone strikes us. But always remember, son, that a man's only got two cheeks. If somebody won't lay off after you've turned 'em both, then you do what you have to. Sometimes you have to hit 'em back. It's a shame when it comes to that, but some people don't seem to get the message any other way."

"Here's one for the funny bone from writer and poet Oscar Wilde: 'Always forgive your enemies—nothing annoys them so much!'" Ms. Hinch squealed with delight. *"I love that quote!"*

Derek's pivotal evening had occurred at the Birmingham City Fest more than a year ago. Having graduated high school, Derek was unguardedly free of the politics of popularity, working part time as a carpenter and paying his way through night school. His overall outlook on life had become more relaxed and optimistic, feeling liberated from the shackling social strata of his former school's tiered class of peers. He had taken the weekend off work to attend the music fest with his friend Opie, who was born with a hearing disability and was there mainly to hang out and see the sights.

Opie was self-employed, and his dogged determination to stake his own claim on life, despite a debilitating handicap, served as the inspiration for Derek to do the same with his carpentry skills. They had been friends since grammar school, and Opie's keen ability to read lips, facilitated by Derek's learned skill at explicitly mouthing his words, allowed the two to develop an unhindered back-and-forth banter that felt as natural as any.

After catching a local blues band, they had stopped at a hotdog stand for a couple of foot-long chili franks when Opie tapped Derek on the shoulder. "Beck Spenz," he said with a grin and a gleam in his eye, pointing over his shoulder.

As Derek took his chili dog from the vendor, he turned to see Becky Spencer approaching from the Budweiser stage. She was tall and tan with a wave of sunny blonde hair. Opie had always maintained a secret crush. Adored by most of the boys in high school, Becky had generally been aloof to Derek but showed a sympathetic interest in Opie—behavior that Derek attributed to a thin sense of guilt she must feel in the face of his handicap. Her otherwise inexplicable attentiveness to the nerd with the hearing aids seemed like an act of condescension to Derek, but Opie never cared, happy to lap up the fawning of a pretty girl.

"Heyyyyy Opie!" she squealed as if greeting a newborn. She hugged him tightly, and he held his dripping dog away from her blouse while winking at Derek.

"Hey Beck!" said Opie, his speech slurred but discernible. "How are you?"

"I'm doing well," she said. She seemed not to notice Derek. "I'm going to school for my teaching certificate. What about you?"

"Work fo mysef," said Opie, nodding proudly.

"I'm sorry?" she said, missing the meaning with his slur.

"He works for himself," said Derek. "He runs his own brick company—Caldwell Masonry. He's a business owner."

Becky regarded Derek briefly, then returned to Opie with genuine surprise. *"Your very own business!"* She said slowly and deliberately to make sure Opie understood her approval. "Why, Opie, I think that's wonderful! I'm so proud of you!"

"That is absolutely wonderful!" came a familiar voice from behind them. The three turned to find Billy Farling and Pierce Mathers emerging from the shifting crowd of festival-goers.

"Everything is wonderful!" cheered Pierce, with a menacing lilt in his voice.

"It's a wonderful life!" jeered Billy.

"Hey, guys, how are you?" greeted Becky.

They each held a can wrapped in a paper bag and smelled strongly of booze. "Becky, why the hell are you hangin' out with these two faggots?" asked Billy.

"Yeah, queers," said Pierce. "Don't you losers have some losing to do?"

Derek reached for some napkins. As he was no longer stuck in school, he was free to relocate his chili dog to a more appetizing area of the festival and leave the two chuckleheads behind.

"Good idea. Get lost," said Billy as Derek gathered his food.

"Guys, be nice," said Becky to Pierce.

"You too, gimpy," said Billy to Opie. "Get out of here. Go catch the short bus."

Then something happened that dramatically changed the social dynamic of those former classmates of Fulton Springs High. Opie told them what he thought.

"Fuh ooh!" said Opie with unfettered spite. Although he

slurred the obscenity, the meaning was clear and his eyes burned through Billy and Pierce.

"What'd you say, retard!" roared Billy, who squared up with Opie. Billy was much larger and cast Opie in a long shadow. He grabbed Opie's chili dog and dumped it onto his chest, mashing the mess all over his clothes. Then he shoved hard and Opie fell over backward onto the asphalt, spilling his drink and cracking his head. While he was down, Billy kicked him in the side.

When Opie opened his watery eyes they were fixed on Becky and trembling with humiliation.

"Billy!" she yelled. "You're such a jerk!"

Derek's ears filled with the shocked gasps of the surrounding crowd. He dropped his food to the ground. Through some strange trick of the mind, Derek did not interpret the shocked reaction of the crowd to be disapproving gasps from passersby disturbed by a fight. Instead, he heard sneers and snickers and taunts and the haunting laughter of a gym full of teenage girls giggling with glee at the sight of a beaten, naked boy. That sound swelled and twisted and bludgeoned his brain and became an earthshaking and irrepressible call to arms. Derek felt like his body was full of fire, and lava would soon fly from his eyes, and he was not conscious of the fact that he had grabbed the heaviest blunt object within reach. His actions were possessed by a demonic whirling dervish of righteous indignation and a violent lust for justice. Since graduating, he had been exercising religiously, growing his muscles, and now he felt an instant infusion of insurmountable confidence as he reared back his sinewy arm, clutching a metal napkin dispenser that had been on the condiment counter of the hot dog stand.

Billy Farling turned just in time to see the sun glare against the shining metal. Derek swung the dispenser with catapultic force into the side of Billy's meaty head, and it crashed with a beautiful bell-like clang that seemed to float above the stunned crowd and ride the wind for miles as a telltale chime of vindication for all the bullied and ostracized individuals who had put up with too much crap, from too many people, for far too long.

Billy staggered momentarily, his eyes rolled back revealing nothing but whites and he toppled like a felled pine.

The next thing Derek knew, he was being cuffed and escorted from the park into the back of a police cruiser. The charge was assault, but Derek never felt a hint of regret.

"Mr. Standish," said Ms. Hinch. *"What are your thoughts on forgiveness? Do you find yourself able to forgive the man with whom you got into the confrontation that led you here?"*

Derek reflected for a moment. *Forgive him?* thought Derek. It was a question he had never considered.

"Maybe," he said. "But first I had to knock him out cold."

***

Frieda Collins was a single letter away from BINGO when the basement door to St. Peter's Cathedral swung open to reveal Officer Farling tapping a church bulletin in his hand. Two officers stood behind him as backup. Farling's chest was puffed out and proud, and dark sunglasses shielded his glare. He glassed the scene of the crime for signs of danger and shook his head in indignant disapproval.

"Bingo," he said in a low, dry voice, his best Clint Eastwood. "Looks like we've got ourselves a crime."

Betsy spun to Frieda with an expression of sheer terror. "It's the fuzz!" she yelled as she   struggled onto her walker and made a painstakingly slow break for the back door.

"It's not wise to advertise an illegal activity right here in the church bulletin," announced Farling as he stepped into the room. "It states right here," he said, raising the folded yellow paper, "Community BINGO, i.e. *gambling*, at six o'clock Tuesday nights in the church basement. Five dollar buy-in, fifteen-dollar pots ... You people are not exactly master criminals, y'know."

Oscar stood up at the back of the room. "Don't you fellas have anything better to do than give us a hard time? We've been having this bingo game every week for 15 years."

Farling's smile curled smugly beneath his heavy moustache. "Well, it sounds like you've been breaking the law for fifteen years, huh?" He glanced at the two officers flanking him and nodded the order: "Confiscate the contraband."

The officers worked their way down the three rows of folding tables, snatching bingo cards from the hands of elderly Catholics who, moments before, had been enjoying the highlight of their week.

When one of the officers took Selby's card, he asked, "Are you serving right now? Or are you protecting?" Selby didn't get an answer.

"This activity will not continue," proclaimed Farling to the room at large. "The church will receive a citation and a fine ... this time ... further indiscretions will result in harsher measures. Please don't force our hand."

He stopped across the table from Frieda and dropped his smile. He extended his hand for her card.

This time it was Frieda who gave the smug grin. "Nice haircut," she said.

Farling's hand flew to his bald spots, still painful, as an

involuntary reflex and he instantly regretted the gesture, which belied the stoic facial expression he was forcing to conceal the grinding of his teeth. He took a long moment to swallow his pride.

"Your card, *please*," he demanded.

Frieda held out the bingo card, but when he tried to grab it she let it flutter to the floor, forcing Farling to chase it clumsily across the room.

He snatched it up and marched angrily toward the door along with his two sidekicks. "You folks better walk softly from now on!" he shouted over his shoulder as he exited the basement. "I'll be keeping an eye on you, and if things get out of sorts, the heavy hammer of the law will drop down upon you." Standing in the doorway, a safe distance from Frieda, he shot her a final cold stare and said, "You got that? The hammer will drop!" And he disappeared out the door along with the Tuesday night fellowship activity for St. Peter's senior citizens.

***

Frank was unloading a delivery of meat at the back of the Bull when Nathan Stevenson approached him, nervously rubbing his temples.

"Hey, Frank. Do you remember those 1,000 signatures I said we needed to get your name on the ballot?"

"I remember," said Frank, short of breath as he stacked the racks of ribs from the refrigeration truck. "We anywhere close?"

"Um. No," said Nathan.

"We've still got about two weeks to find 'em," Frank said.

"We'll get it done."

Nathan winced. "Actually, you've got 'til Friday. The mayor's not exactly pleased with your candidacy, so they moved up the date at last night's council meeting."

Frank stopped unloading the truck. He felt a sharp pain in the back of his neck. He tossed the ribs he was holding onto the freezer pile.

"That figures," he said, clapping off his hands. "Where do we stand right now?"

"Three hundred-twelve." Nathan signed the number with his fingers, three-one-two.

"How do we get this done?"

Nathan shrugged with his palms in the air, "Seems to me that given the tight time frame, the only way to hack it is with feet on the street."

The call for door-to-door foot soldiers in search of signatures spread like fire on dry grass, and volunteers were soon showing up by the car-load to receive their photocopied signature sheets and canvas their neighborhoods.

Never one to gather dust, Frank headed out to do his own soliciting. He had an awkward start. The task required disturbing people in their homes to ask for a favor. Frank felt like a bother, but he explained why he was running for office: To represent the people and their individual freedoms, not certain special interests or the growth of government.

"Yeah, yeah, yeah," said one elderly gentleman who seemed annoyed to have Frank rap on his storm door. "I've heard that spiel before. *'I'll be different. I won't get into office and turn into another crook like all the others,'*" he mocked in an oddly infantile voice. "Everybody claims to have the people's interest in mind until they win an election, then they ditch their principles. Ain't it funny how once a candidate's in office, 'the people' are no longer important— reelection is. Whatever it takes to get reelected, that becomes priority number one, and that's why I don't trust any stinking politicians."

"You've got a point, sir. That's why I won't be seeking reelection. I'll be a one-termer." Frank was only riffing, but as he made that promise it occurred to him that it might actually be an effective strategy. "I just want to stop this mayor from doing any more damage to my hometown, correct some of the things I feel he's gotten wrong, and then go back to work at my barbecue joint. After me, somebody else can step in, 'cause I'm not interested in being a career politician."

The man cocked his head with a quizzical expression. He stuck a finger in his ear and jostled it around.

"Come again?" he said.

"Sir, I won't be seeking reelection. I think you hit the nail on the head. I think the problem with our government is exactly what you said. Politicians run on promises to fight for the people, but once they get into office they make compromises in order to play the political game and have a good shot at reelection. They make deals with the devil for greater political influence in the future. I figure that limiting myself to only a single term as mayor should remove all such temptation."

"Really?" The man seemed intrigued. "One term?"

"I want to assure the voters as a matter of record that the people of Fulton Springs will remain more important to me than any election in the future. It's a way of immunizing myself. I'm insulating myself from the corruption of the office. To be honest, I don't really want to run in this upcoming election, but I feel like somebody needs to stop the mayor. He's running roughshod over anybody who gets in his way, business owners and townsfolk included."

"Yeah, he's a jackass," said the man.

"Anyway, I'm not exactly asking for your vote today. But I do need a thousand signatures by Friday, just so I can put my name on the ballot."

"Hand me your sheet there," said the man. He scribbled down the name Fred Matthews. "Tell me, Mr. Standish. What you just told me about running for only one term, in order to keep yourself honest … Is that something that you'd be willing to state publicly? To make part of your campaign platform? The one-term mayor?"

"I sure would," said Frank. "Because I'd vote for that candidate."

"Yeah," said Mr. Matthews. "I think I would, too. Good luck, Sonny."

***

"Sir, Frank Standish got the signatures he needed," said Pierce Mathers as he stepped into the mayor's office.

A look of pain flashed over Cornelius's face when he heard this. "Dammit, I thought we put a lid on this thing when we moved the deadline!"

"That was the plan, sir. But this man can act fast, and he's apparently got a lot of support." Mathers had recently re-styled his hair with some slick-back gel, which accentuated the reptilian shape of his face. The mayor considered that the boy was maturing into his adult form.

"Support?" scoffed the mayor. "Half the community attends

the First Baptist! My church! I've got their votes locked up! So who the hell is supporting *him?*"

"It appears to be the other half of the community. He's got a built-in fan base at that bar of his, plus he's got name recognition from his former racing career. Farling's stunt at St. Peter's pretty much locked up the Catholic vote in favor of Standish. And word has it that he's been out meeting the people face to face, spreading the gospel, so to speak." Mathers cringed at his poor choice of words

"Spreading the gospel!" screamed Cornelius. "He can't *spread the gospel!* I *spread the gospel!* I'm Reverend Davenport Cornelius!" He stood and stomped around the office in a fury, slamming books and slapping a pile of papers to the floor. "Face to face, *my foot!* I've got years of face-to-face time with these people under my belt. I've got a history, and he wants to take it all away!"

"I'm afraid there's more bad news," said Mathers, retreating to the far corner of the room. The mayor's face was beet-red and swollen, and Mathers worried that more stress might make his head explode in a mist of blood. "Word is spreading about the fishing ban."

The mayor did not explode; recognizing the threat, he merely trembled, gulped down the rage and concentrated on settling his blood pressure. Calmer, he returned to his chair.

"But we haven't banned fishing yet," said Cornelius, more restrained. "That doesn't come until well after the next election."

"There's been a leak. Right now, of course, the ban is just a rumor because there's nobody but us to confirm it. And we haven't confirmed it."

"So what's the problem?"

"Rumors are still destructive, sir. This is Alabama and there are a lot of serious fresh-water anglers who vote. If they even suspect that you're going to close the Six Mile, they'll start peeling away support."

"How big could the 'fishing lobby' be? That 'Free the Fish' check was big money. I can't undo our agreement at this point. I need that money. It's like ammunition against Standish. It's going to buy me air time on the local TV networks."

"Fair enough," said Mathers. "I just wanted to put the issue on your radar screen. My main concern is First Baptist. That's your core voting bloc, and there are a lot of outdoor-types who attend. You don't want cracks in your base due to unhappy fishermen."

The Mayor cracked his knuckles. "No, I don't, but it's kind of a moot point right now. We'll just have to hope for the best. They're still my congregation after all, and the Lord will watch over me."

Pierce Mathers, a non-believer, lost a little more respect for the mayor every time he invoked God to aid his political ambitions. Mathers had no pretension as to his personal greed for political power; he was out to gain money and influence and had always seen those simple pursuits as his goal in life. Cornelius behaved in the same self-serving manner with every opportunity to do so, but at the same time acted as if his decisions were made in the name of God and goodness. Mathers chalked the mayor's false front up to guilt—the mayor's feeble attempt to justify his behavior by calling it holy—a lame effort to ease the cognitive dissonance he suffered from preaching the Gospel and living a lie. Mathers did not suffer the double-think, and was happy to climb a pile of bodies without a shred of remorse, as long as it meant he was moving up in the world.

"How fond are you of salt?" asked Mathers.

"Salt?" asked Mayor Cornelius as he sipped his stale coffee. "How do you mean?"

"Salt, the spice of life," he said. "Potato chips, French fries, you know ... salt. What do you think of a city-wide mandate on limiting salt in restaurants to reduce the likelihood of heart disease among the residents."

"Salt tastes good," said Cornelius. "I like salt. Limit it? Why would I do a thing like that?"

"Salt is a serious health risk. Too much salt is bad for you."

The mayor shrugged. "So what?"

"I think it's reasonable for the city to regulate the salt intake of its citizens for the sake of public health and safety."

This did not interest the mayor, who only sighed and rubbed his eyes, slumping down further into his plush, leather chair. "I think we have enough irons in the fire at this point, and frankly I don't see why the mayor's office would be interested in the salt intake of the citizens."

"I thought you'd find less interest in the salt issue than you would in the salt lobby. Specifically, the Alabama Salt Reduction Task Force. They've got deep pockets, and my sources suggest they'd be willing to cut a sizable check to your campaign fund in exchange for a little favorable city legislation down the line."

The mayor perked up and rose to his feet. "I see. Tell me more."

Pierce flipped a page on his legal pad and read studiously from his notes. "The majority of Americans consume at least a teaspoon and a half of sodium a day, which is more than twice what our bodies need. This excess salt raises blood pressure and with it the risk of heart attack and stroke. The Alabama Salt Reduction Task Force recognizes the mayor's office doesn't have the authority to impose limits on salt content in packaged food—the task force's ultimate goal—but they would like to see some mandated restraint on the ingredients of restaurant food prepared here in Fulton Springs. The Task Force endorses a 60-percent mandatory reduction for restaurant ingredients. They'd like to use our city as a model for more towns to follow."

The mayor pontificated. "So, all we have to do is pass a law that restricts salt content in restaurant foods?"

"Basically, yes," said Pierce. "Sir, the public at large has proven unwilling to or incapable of making sound dietary decisions to encourage a healthy lifestyle, and I feel that under these circumstances it's the government's role to make these decisions for the public."

"And we'd get a wad of money for my campaign effort?"

"That's the gist of it, sir. But we'll need to keep the plan quiet until after the election." Pierce was certain that he had scored some points.

Cornelius's face brightened like he had switched on the high beams. "Well, since it's for the good of the people, consider it done," he said with a giddy smile. "Piercey, make the necessary phone calls."

The mayor then busied himself with tidying his desk and collecting the strewn papers from the floor. This was his self-conscious attempt to regain an air of professionalism after the tantrum in front of his assistant.

"Keep me posted on your progress with the salt folks," he said to Pierce as he grabbed his briefcase and headed for the door. "I'm going home for the day."

***

The squealing guitars and bowling-ball bass line of his favorite hardcore punk band roared from Derek's car speakers as he rounded a sharp curve in his Mustang. Tonight he was feeling alive and purposeful. He had always harbored what he felt was a healthy disdain for authority, but it was an unfocused, scattershot sort of animosity fueled by adolescent hormones. He directed his silent scorn at all instances of society's propensity for groupthink and conformity. He did not understand why so many people so readily relinquished their independent thought in order to assimilate to the rules and ideas of the treasured "people of influence," whether those people be teachers, principals, movie stars or the most popular kids in the clique. Having graduated from the confines of high school and become part of the convoluted world of jobs, laws, taxes and government edicts, he realized that the same herd mentality that so often dictated high school culture also plagued the "adult" society at large. And, while working at The Bull and witnessing his father's struggle with city officials and their misguided mandates, which most of the other businesses suffered like the caning of a Singapore thief, his disdain for people's flaccid acceptance of over-reaching authority was gaining clarity. He was proud his father had fought back. His dad's struggles helped Derek pinpoint the source of his angst and fixate a face upon it, focusing his teenage rage and crystallizing it into something potentially more constructive—an ideology.

He had once seen *The Wild One* on TV, a movie in which someone had asked Marlon Brando's character, "What are you rebelling against?" Brando answered, "Whadda you got?" That exchange had echoed with Derek for years. He loved its open-ended nature, which committed to nothing and left the countless ills of the world wide open as the object of his contempt. But as he entered his twenties, the haze of his dissatisfaction had grown more refined. If that question were to be posed to him today, Derek would respond, "I'm rebelling against any attack on my individual liberties," and then spit on the ground for dramatic effect.

He viewed the city's unending restrictions and regulations directed at The Bull to be an assault on his father's liberty, a personal attack on his family, on their means of making a living and on what Derek considered to be the American way of life. It was an attack that would not go unchecked.

Derek parked the Mustang and switched off the ignition, silencing the explosive guitar assault on his eardrums. He slid out of the car and crept over the interstate overpass where he began to anchor the weights of the new banner to the concrete balusters of the bridge. The night was calm and quiet, except for the crickets and the occasional passing car. He worked from one end to the other, pulling each knot tightly in the twine. When it was all secure, he jogged from one end to the other, flipping the sign over the bridge where it fell open, screaming its message at any passing car in tall, dark red letters:

"We Will Not Do What They Want or Do What They Say"

Derek fired up the Mustang, stabbed the gas and steered homeward.

***

Everybody who knew him agreed — Rocky Jones was one cool cat. Fulton Springs' very own barbecue legend was widely regarded as a local treasure as much for his impeccable smoked pork ribs and beef brisket as for his laidback, easygoing manner. He had a reputation as a generous man who had been subjected to a long spell of devastating bad luck only to come out of that dark tunnel smiling. Seven years earlier he was proprietor of his own establishment called

Rocky's Place located two miles up the road from The Bull, which served his grilled meats to eager customers who would travel from miles away. Tragically, there was an after-hours fire while his twelve-year old daughter and her fourteen-year old cousin were taking inventory. They were earning money for a trip to the shopping mall. Rocky was 10 miles away, picking up supplies when it happened. Both girls were overcome with smoke inhalation and perished. The building burned to the ground.

Rocky was devastated, a broken man, virtually inconsolable for months and stuck in a fathoms-deep mire of melancholia. Then, fate twisted the knife. With the closing of his business, his family's health insurance had lapsed, right at the time his wife discovered she had cancer. Rather than re-building Rocky's Place, the insurance settlement from the fire went to her medical treatments. The money gradually bled away, along with Loretta Jones' health. She succumbed to her illness, and Rocky became a living cadaver, a husk of a man who refused to leave his house or answer the phone as the bills piled high.

Eventually, word of Rocky's depression made it to Frank, who had been made aware of the man's trials and tribulations courtesy of the small town gossip mill. Frank visited Rocky at his home, and having been a devout fan of his skill on the grill, made him an offer: He would expand the Bull's hamburger-and-hot dog menu into a full-fledged, slow-smoked barbecue powerhouse. And he wanted Rocky to captain the ship. Rocky found a renewed calling, a new set of friends and a new lease on life. His disposition defrosted with the heat of the charcoals, and before long he was back to his old, happy, easygoing self—a real cool cat.

That's why Frank knew there was a problem when he noticed Rocky's sullen cheeks and worried brow as he chopped the rib racks for the evening prep.

"What's the bee in your bonnet, Rock?" Frank asked as he strolled into the kitchen.

Rocky stopped what he was doing and looked up. "I've been waiting on you to show up. You heard the rumors? 'Bout what the mayor's got up his sleeve?"

Frank's eyes felt instantly heavy. He blinked hard and braced himself. "What now?"

"No more taste," said Rocky. "No more flavor. No more barbecue—none worth eatin', anyway. They're gonna take the *salt* out of our *food*, Frank. Can you believe that?" Rocky realized he was shaking his butcher knife as he talked. He put it down.

"What are you talking about, Rock?"

Rocky raised his eyebrows and returned to his work. "Hey, I'm just tellin' you what I heard, boss. Mama Cooper told me, and she heard it from her niece who answers phones for city hall. 'Cording to her, the mayor's gettin' a big sack of money for his election if he promises to keep salt off the menu here in the city. What you think that's gonna do to our barbecue business? Does salt-free barbecue sound good to you?"

"Salt?"

"*Salt!*" said Rocky. "I can't make my sauce without salt, boss. Can you believe that? Of all the silly things ... we ain't forcin' anybody to eat salt. For cryin' out loud, if you don't want salt, don't eat it. Eat something else. Eat an apple. Why they gotta be makin' everything *illegal*? Salt ain't a crime!" The cool cat had his hair raised.

"Don't worry about it. I'll look into it."

"This is gonna kill off Mama Cooper's business, too. She's fit to be tied," said Rocky. Mama Cooper was an old friend of Rocky's who ran a soul food restaurant over on Tarrant Street. "Flavor," said

Rock. "Who wants to go through life without any flavor?"

"Salt …" Frank quietly repeated to himself. The word hung on his tongue and it was bitter.

***

"Son, you know you can count on my full support," said Edna Standish to Frank from across her kitchen table where they shared a coffee. "I trust you. The town trusts you. Public service should be just what it sounds like—serving the public, not serving your next campaign ambitions." She adjusted the scarf that wrapped her head. "There's a strong contingent out there that believes in strict term limits for political figures, and it sounds like you're imposing your own. That's a stance I think would resonate with a lot of people, and one campaign promise that I don't think I've heard before."

"That's the game plan, I guess," said Frank. "Introduce some fresh ideas. I just want to be sure that what I'm doing is right. That it's right for Fulton Springs."

Frank and his mother sat at her dining room table, sharing a bagel and conversation, as was their weekly Saturday morning ritual. He treasured these quiet, private moments they spent together, dreading the day she would no longer be there.

"You're a good boy, Frank. Have you asked God if this is His plan for you?"

Frank peered up from his cup. He nodded. "Yes," he said, and it was true. Frank could be terse, gruff and downright standoffish, but he was quietly spiritual in his own private way. "Fancy and I, we prayed together. But I'm not sure I've heard an answer from Him.

Everyone else seems supportive. In fact, there seems to be a real fire in the belly of my supporters, more than I've ever seen in a local race around here. But I'm not sure I've got the seal of approval from The Man Upstairs. I don't feel like I've had that lightning-bolt moment where He says to me: This is my design."

His mother smiled. She had soft, fair skin that defied her age and poor health, but Frank could tell she was not feeling well. Her color was pale. She would always deny it to spare his feelings, but he knew the truth.

"What you're worried about reminds me of a joke someone told me at the treatment center," smiled his mother. She set her mug down and adjusted the scarf that wrapped her head. "It goes like this … there's a poor man whose home is threatened by a flood. As the rain begins, his neighbors ask him to get in their car so they can drive him to safety. The man says, 'No, thank you. God will protect me,' and he refuses the ride. The neighbors drive away as the water continues to rise. The flood becomes waist deep, and another neighbor rows by in a canoe, offering to rescue the poor man. 'No, thank you. God will protect me,' says the man. So, the neighbor rows away. The water continues to rise, so the man climbs onto his roof to escape it. Finally a helicopter arrives, which lowers a ladder to the man, and the rescue workers shout to him, 'Climb aboard to safety!' The man refuses, saying 'No, thank you. God will protect me.' So the helicopter flies away. The water rises further and the man eventually drowns. At the gates of heaven, he meets his maker. 'God, I had faith in you! You let me drown! Why didn't you protect me?' And God's reply to him was: 'I sent you a car, a boat and a helicopter, what more did you want?'"

Frank smiled and immediately understood. He had already heard the joke, but its meaning was poignant.

"Maybe all that lively support you're enjoying is God's way of telling you He approves."

In his eyes, his mother was a perfect creature in an imperfect world, an angel in a land of cancers. He could never repay her wisdom, generosity and guidance, but he strove to pass the same values on to his children as his only means of recompense. And that's all she ever wanted.

***

Mayor Davenport Cornelius's afternoon was about to go from sunny to showers in a matter of seconds.

He had spent the day taping his new campaign advertisement at a Birmingham television studio, and he was swollen with satisfaction. The masterful way his script had heralded his fine commercial accomplishments for the city, while also condemning the sinful nature of his political opponent, was sure to deal a double-barreled blow that would level his competition and end any threat to his reelection bid. This was his first foray into televised campaign ads; it had never before been necessary. But this was a venue the mayor felt confident he could monopolize, given the high cost of television production and air time. He would simply outspend his opponent. The strategy was to campaign so heavily in such expensive, high-profile arenas, where Standish could not afford to compete, that the mayor would essentially obscure the competing point of view.

Cornelius was beaming as he steered the car into his reserved parking space at the rear of city hall, singing along to a gospel CD in his car stereo. He was practically dancing in his seat as he unbuckled his distressed seatbelt and pulled the keys from the ignition. He gathered his phone and wallet from the passenger seat, unaware of the two long shadows that passed quickly alongside his sedan. The shadows were lying in wait as he pulled the handle to the car door. The moment it was ajar, one of the shadows flung it open.

The mayor was staring down the barrel of a 9-millimeter Glock handgun. He was instantly petrified, and dared not take his eyes off the muzzle for fear that doing so might somehow trigger it to fire. He did not know who was pointing the gun at him, but the peripheral shapes suggested it was two individuals wearing some sort of ski masks.

"Give us your money you fat mother—"

The mayor didn't hear the rest; he seized up like a shoddy engine. Upon hearing the words, his body revolted with an uncontrollable head-to-toe muscle spasm. His face contorted into a wrinkled, red mass and he completely vacated his bowels, then fainted.

"Oh, man!" said one of the muggers. "He just crapped himself!"

"Grab the wallet and phone—*let's go!*"

***

"A one-term candidate. A *deliberate* one-term candidate!" boomed Marty Madigan into his mic. "I've been covering politics on the radio for a long time, but I do believe this is the first I've ever heard of a candidate running on a platform where he refuses to run for a second term. I repeat: This man says if he is elected, he will *refuse to run* for a second term. A self-imposed term limit! I love it!

"I guess there is something new under the sun, and while I don't typically give a lot of our valuable air time to these small-time local elections, word of this man's particular campaign strategy sparked my interest. His name is Frank Standish, and you may remember him from his effort to rehab a house condemned by the City of Fulton Springs in order to save a friend's home. Well, he's riding that wave of publicity right into the campaign season, taking on the political establishment, and we have him in studio to pick his brain. Mr. Standish, welcome to the Marty Madigan Show."

"Thanks for having me, Mr. Madigan," said Frank. "I do appreciate the publicity. My campaign doesn't have quite the budget of our current mayor, so I'm happy to come on the air and plead my case."

"Well, we're happy to have you—and call me Marty, please."

"If you call me Frank." He had not been inside a radio station since his days as a driver. Electronic equipment was everywhere, and the microphones and control booths looked much more sophisticated than he remembered.

"Frank, let's get a little background on you. You were a race-car driver of note in your younger years, correct?"

"I was far from famous, but I guess some of the locals might have taken note."

"And now, you're proprietor of a bar?"

"It's got a bar in it, yes. It's called The Bull, but it's not some kind of seedy dive. It's a barbecue restaurant, helmed by Rocky Jones, the best grill-master in the South, as far as I'm concerned. We've got a real all-inclusive type of family atmosphere. Everybody's welcome to come enjoy good food and good company."

"So, you were a racecar driver, became a business man, and now you're entering the world of politics?"

"I was fairly successful at my first two jobs. Time for something new."

"What inspired this run for office?"

"Big government. Corrupt government that negatively affects my business, my life and the lives of others in my community."

"You say corrupt, but that's a strong word. Are you alleging any sort of illegal activity on behalf of the current mayor?"

"Illegal? I've got no proof of that. *Improper?* Yes, in my estimation the current city officials do little more than line their own pockets and those of their special interests in an effort to maintain and grow the power they currently hold. There are a lot of ways to screw the electorate within the confines of the law. And in doing so, the individual liberties of the citizens of Fulton Springs are under constant attack."

"Give me some specific examples."

"Out-of-control tax increases. I've brought figures if you'd like to see them. Under this mayor's leadership taxes on individuals and business owners have been raised 14 different times."

"Taxes … *yawn* … With all due respect, complaining about taxes is passé. Been there, done that. Every political seems to do it," said Madigan. "Tell me something new."

"Under this mayor's leadership, you apparently aren't free to live in a house that needs a little work—or if it's sitting in the way of a shopping mall. He calls it eminent domain, but this mayor is confiscating property for private profit, not for the public good. That's the reason I was on your show the last time.

"What's more, we'll soon no longer be allowed to fish in Six Mile Creek. The mayor made a new law for some sort of fish conservation group that's worried about the extinction of something called a 'spunk' minnow. I've never even heard of a spunk minnow.

"His latest crusade: The senior citizens at the Catholic church can no longer play Bingo. The City of Fulton Springs has put a stop to that great evil. Legal adults aren't free to gamble in any way. Legal adults are not free to have an alcoholic beverage unless they do so according to the mayor's schedule. These days, people aren't free to smoke in their own private establishment, because his majesty does not approve of such things. Don't think that just because you own your business means you make the rules. In Fulton Springs, the mayor makes the rules.

"And now that he's got a challenger—me—he's really breaking out the big guns, taking all sorts of money from all sorts of lobbies. In other words, he'll have debts to pay if he's reelected."

"Debts to pay? Give us examples," said Madigan.

"He pays them with political favors. Here's what's on his agenda—that I know of—Mayor Davenport Cornelius will regulate salt intake in restaurants. That'll pay off the anti-salt lobby that cut his campaign a check. Evidently he doesn't think we're smart enough to make our own dietary decisions, so he'll take away the people's freedom to do so." Frank had not formally prepared for the interview, but found that when he spoke from the gut, the words seemed to fall into place.

"I agree that it's none of the government's business, but how would you counter the argument?" asked Madigan. "I mean, to play the devil's advocate, it's been proven that too much salt intake is unhealthy."

"So what?" said Frank. "Then, don't eat too much salt. You have the freedom of choice, to eat or not eat salty foods. Eat at The Bull one day, have a salad the next. It's about choice, moderation and personal responsibility. Nobody's shoving barbecue down your throat the way this jackass shoves his legislation down ours."

"What about smoking? Some people may not want to eat in a restaurant that has a smoking section."

"Then don't eat there. You have the choice not to do so. What about the people who do want to eat in an establishment where they can have a cigarette? He's taking away their choice, and my choice to offer that service. Simply put, freedom of choice is being restricted. I say, let the free market decide. I may lose the business of non-smokers but gain the business of smokers. This way, a restaurant that caters to a strictly non-smoking crowd can take advantage of that customer base. See the beauty of it? It's self-regulating, and nobody's freedom gets compromised. And, for the record, I have both a smoking and non-smoking section at The Bull."

"As a single-term mayor, do you think you can correct all these things that you believe are wrong?"

"Yes, I do. A lot of 'em, anyway. I'll eliminate any of the mayor's new regulations that infringe on the personal liberties of the citizens. I'll pass a law protecting the property rights of homeowners from confiscation for private interest. And I'll audit the city budget to see just where our money is being spent. I believe in fiscal restraint. Will those changes stay in place after my tenure? That remains to be seen. We'll have to see who fills my shoes, if I'm lucky enough to be elected mayor. But I hope I'll set an example for those who might follow.

"I always default to freedom," said Frank. "This is supposed to be the Land of the Free. Let's keep it that way. What scares me the most is the lazy acceptance of the citizens who put up with all these top-down mandates about their lifestyles. To keep quiet is to accept it. The current mayor counts on his citizens being too distracted or uninformed to put a stop to his nonsense. He wants our silence, because it makes things easy for him. He interprets it as approval. I'm breaking that silence."

"So you see yourself as a defender of freedom," said Madigan.

Frank thought for a moment "You have a dramatic way of wording things, Mr. Madigan."

"Marty, please."

"But I suppose I do, in a small way. Look, I don't want to infringe upon anyone else's right to live however they see fit. I just want to get intrusive government out of the lives of the Fulton Springs citizens. To roll back all these new rules, the latest of which are in place just to finance the mayor's reelection campaign. In other words, his latest round of rules and regulations has nothing to do with genuine philosophy or principles, but selfishness—the need to save his own skin ..."

Frank paused to collect his thoughts. "You know, the other day I saw a big sign hanging off an I-65 overpass," he said. "It read: We Will Not Do What They Want or Do What They Say. I liked that sign. My sentiments exactly."

"Frankly, you seem to be running a pretty caustic, negative campaign against the existing mayor," said Madigan. "You make a lot of charges. A lot of people don't appreciate negative campaigns."

"Well, I'm ticked off, and so are a lot of other people. The only things I'm 'negative' about are cronyism, wasted tax dollars and the attacks on individual liberties. If you want me to be positive about those propositions, then you've got the wrong guy. Vote for Cornelius if that's your bag. He'll give you enough nanny-state government to choke on."

"Why the decision to run on a 'single-term' platform?" asked Madigan. "If you do a great job, the public may want to re-elect you."

"I'm vowing not to run for a second term for the simple reason that it removes any temptation—both real and perceived—to compromise my beliefs in order to further my political career. I don't want to further my political career, so why would I compromise my principles? It's assurance I'm offering to the voting public that they can trust me. And once I'm in office, it makes it pointless for lobbyists to bait me with campaign donations. I see this strategy as instilling a level of honesty and accountability that's been missing from our political system for a long time. I only want to serve the citizens of Fulton Springs according to my principles, and then let someone else—hopefully with similar views—take the reins and protect our freedoms."

"You're certainly an interesting man, Mr. Standish."

"I think this will be an interesting race."

***

The TV screen in Frank's living room held the image of an American flag whipping in the wind. The flag dissolved into a still portrait of two hands folded in prayer as a symphonic chorus of "My Country Tis of Thee" swelled in the background. The screen faded to white, and then Reverend Cornelius appeared, fire-branding a sermon to an attentive congregation of hundreds.

"For nearly a decade Mayor Davenport Cornelius has led the City of Fulton Springs into times of growth and prosperity," assured the fatherly voice of an unseen narrator. "A friend of business and church alike, Cornelius first gained notoriety as the trusted patriarch of the Fulton Springs Baptist Church. His reputation for impeccable moral character, traditional values and a common sense approach to leadership inspired his nomination to the office, and Fulton Springs has enjoyed unprecedented success ever since." The camera panned over the construction zone of the new shopping center. Then the screen darkened, followed by a booming crash of thunder.

"—But the city now faces a new challenge..." the narrator's voice hardened into the dire tone of a primetime police procedural. "...A challenge in the form of greedy, profit-centered politics. Mayoral challenger and honky-tonk bar owner, Frank Standish, has money on his mind. He doesn't care about drunk driving..." *The sound effect of screeching tires punctuated the sentence. An extreme close-up of a crying baby with the sound of shattering glass.* "He just wants to sell his alcohol! Frank Standish doesn't care about lung cancer." *An elderly man in a wheelchair, gasping into a respirator.* "He wants to roll back the city's smoking ban—even where our children eat!" *Stock footage of child in a high-chair, screaming.*

"Frank Standish has even been charged with operating an illegal gambling operation, right out of his bar... Is this the kind of moral leadership we need in Fulton Springs?" *Stock footage of a Las Vegas casino.*

A studio shot of Reverend Dave appeared on the screen in soft focus, where he sat at a large wooden desk with an open Bible before him. "I'm Davenport Cornelius," he said over the soft sound of children singing hymns. "I believe in faith and family values, and I'd be honored if you'd vote for me to serve another term as your mayor. Let's keep Fulton Springs moving in the right direction."

***

Every city in the world has a criminal element. Shane Painter and Terence "T.B." Benson were proud to fill those shoes in Fulton Springs. They were petty crooks, and versed in such dubious crafts as stealing medication and ripping off air-conditioning units to sell the copper wire as scrap. Some families around town had been known to go to sleep with central air conditioning, but then wake up without it. Trashing a $3,000 air conditioner could net about $50 for the copper. However, the routine was getting dull for the enterprising duo, so they were progressing to bolder crimes like armed robbery of the mayor in the city hall parking lot.

"See, man, look at this," said Shane, handing the mayor's stolen smart phone to T.B. He had logged onto the official website of the City of Fulton Springs. The two were sitting in a do-it-yourself carwash lot, sipping cans of malt liquor and waiting for their meth dealer. "This is what I was talkin' about. They're gonna take people's guns away. No concealed carry permits allowed. And, if you got a business in the F-Spring, you gotta get rid of any firearms by the end of next week. It's a 'new ordinance' by the city. See, it says it right there on the internet. 'In the interest of public safety ...'"

"Damn," said T.B., squinting to read the wording on the 3-inch phone screen. "You're right. They're gonna disarm these fools. I can't believe they advertise it like that. Stupid."

"Stupid, for them. Good for us." Shane tilted up his can, and the booze ran sloppily down his chin, its pungent odor filling the car.

"Yeah, good for us," said T.B. "We're gonna catch these fools sleepin' and unarmed, and gank us some money."

"You know that's true. By next Friday night, anybody 'round here with a cash register won't have a gun to guard it. So we'll lighten their load for 'em."

***

For the past week the city hall bulletin board on Main Street had screamed only two words: GUNS KILL!

It was Mayor Cornelius's personal declaration of war on any firearm that he could touch through the influence of his office. From the moment he awoke in his soiled britches, with Pierce Mathers, Officer Farling and his other lackeys encircling him like curious vultures, he clearly saw the inherent evil in guns. It was a gun that had dealt him this humiliating blow. He resolved that without the availability of guns, there would be no way for such hoodlums to physically harm him. A gun ban would safeguard him from this heretofore unseen weakness in his empire. For years he had been blind, taking no heed of such a deadly force at the ready disposal of the untrustworthy and intrinsically sinful commoners. The mayor had let his guard down, and the savages had behaved savagely.

Within 24 hours of the mugging, the mayor had placed all the necessary phone calls to set his plan in motion. The gun ban was announced with zero fanfare at a sparsely attended city council meeting and, as there was no city newspaper in existence, the news was publicized on the City of Fulton Springs website. The city's website suffered a rich tradition of receiving no visitors whatsoever, but as word of the new law spread like oil on a carport slab, it was experiencing an unprecedented surge in traffic from people in need of an official source to verify the story.

Even among Cornelius's faithful flock of First Baptist followers, the voting public was reacting with a resentful backlash.

The rabble had been roused, and many of the reverend's usual supporters were quietly vowing to shift their vote to anyone who opposed The Big Gun Grab, as it came to be known.

Cornelius was unwavering, and took self-righteous solace in the idea that his decision was indeed in the best interest of the health and well-being of Fulton Springs' fine citizens. Furthermore, the thousands of dollars contributed to his campaign coffers by Citizens for a Peaceful Public, a well-financed anti-gun advocacy group, would certainly help seal his reelection bid.

"But you've already lost the fishermen," said Mathers, considering the mayor's campaign strategy. "Now you're losing the hunters, the outdoorsmen and even the conceal-carry nuts. I know you think these are marginal voters, but don't forget that we're in the Deep South. Your voters may have a loyalty to God and their church, but their guns aren't far behind. You keep pushing away your voting block and your congregation might start to question their faith ... in you."

The mayor launched from his chair where he'd been massaging his temples from a pounding headache. "Son, don't *you* try to tell *me* how to mount a political campaign!" he bellowed, spittle flicking off his lips. "I was winning elections while you were still suckin' udders! I know what the hell I'm doing. I know how to calculate the people's response! And I know something very important that you seem to be overlooking!"

The mayor stomped across the office to his private bathroom and opened his fly to relieve himself. He didn't bother to shut the door, and the office was filled with the sound of splashing urine.

"What?" said Pierce loudly over the noise. "What is it that I'm overlooking?"

The reverend finished his business and washed his hands

before exiting the bathroom holding a wad of paper towels. "People are stupid," said the mayor as he chunked the paper into the trash. "Really stupid and easily distracted. All I've got to do is get through this election in one piece, then I'm golden."

"You're hoping they'll just forget how you pissed them off?"

"Not just hoping," said the mayor. "I know they'll forget. A lot of them, anyway. Some will even remember what I did, but forget that they're mad about it. And some will stay mad, but I'm pretty sure I can absorb the collateral losses. The anti-gun money is enough to bankroll some more TV commercials, the TV commercials will nail down some more votes, and the support that I gain will offset anything I lose. See how it works?"

"You sound pretty confident, sir."

"I am confident, kid," said the reverend, popping a couple of aspirin. "You see, people are simple. They get distracted with their lives, with a singing competition on TV, with football season, with video games. These are the things that matter to people today, not politics and local government. As long as you don't rock the boat too much, they won't take notice. And, those who do notice will usually forget by the end of the election cycle—if they even show up to vote. The trick is to nudge the public just a little at a time so they don't wise up to what's really going on, to who is really pulling the strings around town. And as long as they stay distracted, you can keep nudging. You can keep turning up the heat, little by little, gradually changing things to suit your interest. That's what public service is all about. That's how it works. It's like that old nursery rhyme about boiling a toad."

"Boiling a what?" said Mathers.

"It's an allegory," said the mayor. He cleared his throat and recited:

"As the water warms the toad, he does not notice
He soon will come to boil but does not know this
They stoke the fire higher as he waits,
Til he's dead and gone, and spread upon a plate."

Mathers' face was blank. "Who eats a toad?"

"I don't know," said the mayor. "You're missing the point."

"With due respect, sir. You might be turning up the heat too quickly. We were supposed to keep the new regulations quiet. Now, everyone knows. The toads are waking up."

"Horsefeathers!" shouted Cornelius, although his voice carried the faint waver of doubt. "Besides, I *have* been quiet. I think this place is bugged. But no matter—the toads will be fine. I told you, voters are dumb."

Pierce saw the mayor's ship springing leaks, with Pierce's future in politics tethered to its mast. He needed to take the helm for the sake of his own career prospects.

***

"Hey, nerd," greeted Nora as she bounded down the stairs into Derek's dim dungeon lair, draped in unfolded clothes, old TV dinner cartons and scattered woodworking tools.

"Hey, dork," he responded from the old couch on which he was settled, staring at the television.

She skipped over and sat on the floor in front of him, helping herself to the bag of chips on the rickety coffee table. Derek absently flipped TV channels with the remote.

"I need to know something," she said.

"What's that?"

"What does moral leadership mean?"

Derek put down the clicker and wrinkled his brow. "Where'd you here that?"

"On a commercial," she said. "They were talking about Dad. Some of the kids at school were, too."

"Really?" Derek sat up. "What'd they say?"

"Different stuff. Sammy Munford said Dad was a bad person."

Nora and her friend Chuck Haveston had been playing checkers at a picnic table during recess. Nora explained how Sammy and his friends were playing dodgeball nearby when a wayward ball bounded toward the table and knocked the checkerboard to the ground in a flurry of black and red chips.

"Crap!" cursed Chuck. Nora gathered the pieces to restart the game while Chuck retrieved the ball and tossed it to the other kids. "Watch what you're doing!" he told Sammy and returned to the table.

"Shut up, dummy," said Sammy, who had a yellow bullet of snot dripping from his nose. "Don't you know her dad is trashing our town?" pointing to Nora. "Don't you watch TV? It's all over the commercials. You shouldn't even be hanging out with her."

Derek was startled at his sister's story. It had not occurred to him that children so easily believed what they saw on TV, and now Nora was being unfairly castigated by one ill-informed kid who was rallying other kids against her.

"What'd you tell him?" asked Derek.

"I told him he was stupid, and that Dad was a good person and was going to be mayor," said Nora. "Then he called me stupid.

Then Chuck told him not to call me stupid. And then Sammy called Chuck stupid, and Chuck pushed him in the mud, and Sammy started crying. They both had to go to time-out."

Derek thought for a moment. "Moral leadership ... is about teaching people to make the right decisions," he said. "And teaching it by example. Don't worry. Dad is a good example of moral leadership. Don't listen to Sammy at school. Sammy is stupid."

"I know," Nora smiled and crammed her mouth full of Doritos.

Derek continued surfing the channels while lost deep in thought. How many others would believe those commercials? Was Sammy's reaction reflective of the sleepy public at large who had allowed Cornelius to rule the town unchecked for so many years? Would the people of Fulton Springs think for themselves and research the candidates independently, or would they simply ingest the mayor's propaganda with the numb nod of apathy?

The playing field for the mayor's race was weighted heavily in favor of Cornelius. The reverend had powerful bargaining chips—campaign promises—to trade with special interests in exchange for financing his television ads. He was out-gunning his father in the critical arena of mainstream media. Derek realized that in the town of Fulton Springs, if there was going to be a revolution, it would not be televised. He shut off the TV.

The next morning, the first bridge that crossed I-65 was adorned with a bright new homemade banner, nearly 20 feet in length. It stated in bold red letters: VOTE FRANK STANDISH FOR FREEDOM.

The second bridge over the interstate carried one as well. VOTE FRANK STANDISH FOR HONESTY.

And the grassy hillside that overlooked the highway from the

West had a banner staked down at each corner. VOTE STANDISH FOR TRUE MORAL LEADERSHIP.

Derek was fresh out of banners.

After the morning rush hour, Officer Art Brookings was dispatched to remove the signage.

***

Friday evening Officer Farling and two backups entered The Bull shortly after the dinner rush had ended. Everyone in the smoking section stubbed out their cigarettes.

"So this is The Big Gun Grab," said Frank.

The local authorities had split into separate task forces, each team paying a visit to the businesses of Fulton Springs to verify compliance with the new gun ordinance. The day was stretching, and Farling's group of officers had procrastinated over making their visit to The Bull, anticipating the usual blowback from its staff and patrons. This was their last stop.

"Come on, Standish, you knew we were coming," said Farling. "Please don't give me any trouble. It's been a long day." A hush had swept over the restaurant, and all eyes were on Frank as though witnessing a Dodge City standoff. Officer Farling was sporting a freshly shaved head, courtesy of Frieda Collins' impromptu hair alterations.

"Trouble?" asked Frank. "Like refusing to relinquish my firearm?"

"Yes," said Farling, "like refusing to relinquish your firearm."

Frank glassed over the officers' uniforms: navy blue standard issue, complete with costume badges. They each wore their service revolvers in a holster.

"You've come to take away my property by force? Isn't that why people arm themselves? To protect themselves from people who try to take their belongings?"

"Don't be cute."

"What if I told you I don't have a gun here?"

"I know you'd be lying. Everybody in town knows you keep a 12-gauge under the counter."

"I see it right now," said one of the other officers who had slyly strolled to a far corner of the restaurant to steal a glance behind the bar. The black barrel of The Bull's last line of defense, "Matilda," was visible atop a stack of Styrofoam to-go cartons, ready for that singular event when all other efforts have failed to keep the peace and the threat of a shot-riddled hide becomes the final resort. That moment had never happened in the history of The Bull, but the possibility always loomed, and Frank was an advocate of being prepared.

"Hand it over," said Farling. "Let's make this easy. After the weapon is processed you can pick it up at the station and take it to your home, but because you failed to rid the premises of the firearm by the deadline, we're going to have to confiscate it."

"What if I say no?"

Farling stared at Frank and sighed heavily. "We'll take it anyway, Standish."

"By force, you mean," said Frank. "Say it. You'll take it by force."

"By any means necessary, Standish. We have the legal authority to do this."

"As far as I know, we've still got a Constitution that protects my right to bear arms."

"And as far as I know, I've got a legal obligation to ensure no firearms are present in public places within the city limits of Fulton Springs. If you want to contest that, then get a lawyer," steamed Farling. "Now give me the damn gun."

"Let me understand this," said Frank. "I've got a right to bear arms, to protect myself not only from criminals, but also from a corrupt government that might threaten my rights. You say you're here to confiscate my gun, to infringe upon my rights, and if I refuse to comply then you will compel me to comply through force of a gun." Frank crossed his arms. "Do I have that right?"

"Except for one thing," said Farling. "If you don't comply, I'll start with a Taser."

***

The Bull was the type of place where people could feel almost too comfortable, which is why later that night Fancy forgot to lock the front door of the bar, despite the fact that business hours were over. Selby had been the last patron in the bar, and Fancy had left him to his T.V. and beer while she started taking stock in the kitchen. When she peeked back in the bar, he had left, so she cut off the lights and television to signal to any passersby that last call had been served. However, she had not locked the door, which was a welcome discovery for Shane Painter and T.B. Benson.

They had parked their car two blocks away. This was the two men's fourth stop of the evening, after having already burglarized Blakewood Electronics, Main Street Hardware and J&M Auto Body.

They viewed the night's escapade as a high reward-to-risk prospect, as the city police had enforced the gun ban earlier that very day, giving Shane and T.B. total confidence that whatever resistance they might face, it would not be armed resistance, so they could hit the henhouse and get away with their skins.

The two crept into the bar and were trying to pry open the cash register drawer when they heard noises coming from the kitchen. Peering through the double-door windows they saw a female, a shapely black woman with a small waist and smooth skin, arranging canned goods on a shelf and jotting notes on a pad of paper. There was a thin, white wire running from her shoulder to her head. She was listening to an MP3 player and humming to the tune, shaking her butt to the beat and completely oblivious to the intruders.

"Let's go," said T.B. "Let's get out of here!"

"Shhh!" hissed Shane. "Shut up a minute!" He stared longingly at the woman. "What's the rush?"

T.B. had a sinking feeling. "We need to go, fool. She could I.D. us"

Shane was transfixed on the woman. He pushed apart the kitchen doors and approached her from behind. T.B. nudged him in the shoulder, but Shane ignored him, drunk and lustful.

When he was just a couple of feet away, Shane pulled a switchblade. As Fancy reached for a box on the upper shelf, he hooked an arm beneath hers and cupped his hand over her mouth. As a reflex, Fancy ducked and shot an elbow behind her, catching Shane in the breadbasket. He expelled air sharply and grabbed her by the hair, bringing the knife to her face.

"Don't you fight me, bitch!" he said, and licked her cheek. Fancy's eyes were all whites and her lips peeled back in disgust. She could smell the acrid odor of his saliva. He slid the knife tip down into her blouse and cut off the top button with a flick of the blade.

Fancy was enraged and terrified, a strong, feisty woman who wanted to castrate this imbecile, but was also mortified of that 5-inch blade and how it could ensure she never saw her daughter again. She pictured Nora's smiling face, and her whole body began to shake violently. He pressed the knife tip to her flesh. Fancy prayed for God's help.

Shane snatched a handful of her shirt and ripped away the rest of the buttons with a single tug.

***

The spattering rain hit the oily blacktop in a shimmer as Frank's headlights crested the hill of Main Street. He was approaching The Bull, closed for the night, where Fancy said she would be working late on inventory. Frank had left the restaurant with a headache and was doubling back after a trip to the drugstore for aspirin. He was in a sore mood, a gloomy funk in which he wanted to wallow alone. The confrontation with police, the pressure of the election, the interference of city officials with his business—were all taking a toll. During those rare times when his spirit would darken to pitch, Frank always preferred solitude, where he could reflect on the situation and forcefully digest whatever negative news was rolling down life's great conveyor belt.

Something darted in front of the Ford. Frank stabbed the brake, bringing the heavy pickup to a sliding halt. Crouched before him was a cat, cast in the full glow of the halogen headlamps. Frank recognized it as the same silver cat that was always hanging around

The Bull. Its metallic coat glistened with beaded water. It occurred to Frank that this was the only cat he had ever encountered that seemed undeterred by rainy weather. Rather than dart away from the idling vehicle, the cat squared up, facing the big, rumbling machine with utter stoicism. The cat cocked its head and appeared to fixate upon Frank, who was visibly obscured by the shining headlamps and the sheets of rain pouring down the windshield. Still, Frank could swear against his better judgment that this cat was in fact returning his look, locking his gaze and then—Frank would never admit this to another soul—but the cat gestured to him. The cat jerked its head in the direction of the restaurant. *Twice!* thought Frank. He turned to the building and then back to the cat. The cat nodded. It licked its paws, and then darted toward The Bull and out of sight.

Frank twisted the steering wheel and plugged the truck into a parking space. He was acting on a silly hunch, but it was an itch that had to be scratched. The lamp overlooking the parking lot cast a soft white glow over the storefront. All other lights were off. He opened the truck door, pulled his jacket over his head and hopped over to the canopy of the Bull's entry, where he hunkered out of the rain to find the right key in his pocket. The silver cat was nowhere to be seen. A shame he's gone, thought Frank, who felt an odd kinship with the cat and was planning to offer it a saucer of meat.

Frank let the heavy door swing closed behind him and shrugged off his jacket, which was dripping all over the floor. The lobby was dark, but Frank saw the seams of light around the double doors of the kitchen, where Fancy was probably itemizing the quantity of supplies on hand. As he hung the jacket on a hat rack, he heard the familiar crash of a pan on tile bang from the kitchen. A dropped dish. It was a racket he heard ten times a week. He walked to the bar to pour a glass of water. Then, he heard another crash.

108

"Honey?" he called into the other room, "you okay?"

"*FRRRRAAAAANNNNNNNNNKKKKKK!*" came screeching from the kitchen with a timbre of terror his ears had never heard. *Fancy!* A sickening sensation slithered, eel-like, up his spine and constricted his heart. His breathing seized.

At that stark instant, he was on the front porch back home as a child, where his father, who played in a bluegrass trio as a hobby, was tuning his old banjo and teaching Frank the procedure. It was a happy memory; his father loved to spend Sunday afternoons with the family. He remembered his dad plucking those old, worn strings while cranking the keys tighter and tighter. The tone pitched sharper with every turn of his fingers—*Ploonk! Plunk! Plunk! Plink!*—until that banjo string could take no more tension and suddenly broke with a final, perfunctory *Pop!* The memory of that sound, the snapping string, embodied Frank's frame of mind at that moment ... *Plink! Plink! ... Pop!*

Frank Standish shot into action.

***

Remarkable for a man of his age, Frank moved with the driven speed and lithe agility of a natural predator. Beneath the cloak of darkness, he rolled over the bar, crouched to the floor and instinctively snatched beneath the counter for Matilda, but found only an empty shelf.

T.B. Benson burst open the double doors of the kitchen with gun in hand, flooding the dark lobby with a column of light. He darted his head from side to side. He had heard a human voice, no doubt about it, but all he saw was shadow, floor and furniture.

Frank's flash-fire memory of the cops' confiscation of his shotgun—momentarily forgotten in the excitement—was like fuel to the furnace as he connected the causal dots to his current situation: a publicized gun ban, the enforced confiscation and The Bull's first-ever criminal invasion all in perfectly logical sequence. And for it all to occur in the rare moments when his wife was left alone at the bar—how foolish he had been—his wife who was likely succumbing to some unspeakable brutality at that very moment while he was hunched behind the bar retrieving no weapon. It was too much for Frank to bear, and something had to break.

T.B. detected movement in the room, somewhere around the bar. This whole night was a stupid idea, he thought. They were not supposed to have found a woman here. They should have left. Shane was out of control, and T.B. had the sick sense that he was going to suffer for it. As he stood with the light at his back, it occurred to T.B. that whoever was in this room could see him, although he could not see them. This gave him the skittish feeling of a prey animal being stalked by a panther. He raised the Glock with unsteady hands.

"Come out so I can see you!" he yelled.

Nothing. Stillness. In that pocket of blackness behind the bar, Frank tightened a white-knuckle grip on the neck of a liquor bottle. It felt half full.

"What the hell's going on out there!" called Shane from the kitchen. Frank heard the muffled cries of his wife.

T.B demanded of the darkness, "Come out now or I'll shoot, mother—"

The beastly vision that charged from the blackness cloaked T.B. with a paralyzing shroud of fear that would haunt his dreams for the rest of his days. This thing could be no man, with all that sprawling white hair, those ravenous teeth and those fiery eyes. It was a wolfman, maybe, but surely no mortal. T.B. instinctively squeezed off two rounds from … two futile, wayward rounds before Frank consumed him.

T.B.'s life forever changed when Frank smashed the bottle into his face with such impact that he hoped it would burst out the back of the thug's skull. T.B.'s body slammed into the wine rack with a shattering crash. When Frank pulled back his fist, only half the bottle remained intact and he drove it forward again, plunging the broken mass blindly into the intruder's head and shoulder vicinity. In the darkness he could not see exactly where the glass shards made purchase, but when he felt the man's knees buckle, he knew his attention could be safely turned to whoever was accosting his wife.

***

Fancy had managed to wrestle away from her assailant and wield an aluminum cookie sheet as a shield. She raised it feebly before her, trembling uncontrollably. Shane Painter's tongue danced around the corners of his salivating mouth. He registered the gunshots but assumed T.B was taking care of business. He advanced on Fancy, slashing the blade through the air as he stormed toward her, forcing her into the far corner of the room.

The double doors of the kitchen burst open, and Fancy's eyes rose to her husband. He stood in the doorway like a fabled white knight. Her legs folded beneath her.

Frank saw Fancy's torn blouse and tear-stained eyes and he raised the pistol that he had wrenched from the grip of the twitching body on the bar floor.

When Shane saw the firearm he began to stammer and stutter, unable to conjure any intelligible words, muttering only strange gibberish like a biblical tongue. He was the fool with a knife at a gunfight, and his ghost-white face revealed his fear. Shane dubiously raised his switchblade and lunged.

Frank had always been trained that if he were ever forced to fire a gun in self-defense, always shoot to kill. He pulled the trigger.

Blood burst from Shane's knee and he fell to one side, screaming in agony. He still clenched the knife and raised it again. Frank pulled the trigger.

The jeans over the man's other knee darkened with blood, and he howled. Frank was not sure if the burglar even realized that he was still wielding a blade. Frank shot him in the hand and one of his fingers fell to the floor with the knife.

Shane looked up from the floor, his face stretched in a ghastly expression of horror and disbelief. Frank raised the gun to the man's head, right over the bridge of the nose. The man's eyes converged on the muzzle. Frank tickled the trigger with his finger. Then he lowered the gun.

Surely, this moron had had enough. Frank turned to Fancy.

Like a copperhead snake, Shane grabbed the knife, swung in a flash and stabbed Frank in the calf.

Frank roared like a beast unleashed. He spun on his heel, reared backward on the other leg and threw the full brunt of his weight behind a heavy black boot that splintered Shane Painter's jaw and ushered him to a realm of deep, desolate silence.

Frank scooped up Fancy and squeezed her tightly. She sobbed into the crook of his neck, and he held her close as her shaking slowly subsided. His eyes welled, and he took comfort in the warmth of her breath and body. He lifted his gaze upward and beyond the ceiling of The Bull, quietly thanking God for his wife's safe delivery.

The knife still protruded from his leg, and as his heart gradually slowed to a comfortable beat, he considered that maybe he should pull it from his calf.

***

The new gun ban was in full effect, and the mayor had the utmost confidence that he and the town would be safer as a result. No guns meant no shootings, he reasoned. But why stop protecting the people there—especially when there was money to be made in doing so?

"A sugar tax, you say?" mused the mayor to an unhealthily thin woman with horn-rimmed glasses and knobby elbows.

"Mayor, obesity is our nation's leading killer, and it is the government's job to set healthy living standards for the people when the people fail to act responsibly."

The mayor self-consciously stretched together his top coat, struggling to fasten a button. He had a physique like a pile of mashed potatoes. "This kind of legislation isn't usually very popular," he said.

"I understand that, Mr. Cornelius, but I also understand that you're facing stiff competition in the upcoming election. I represent a firm that is willing to infuse your campaign with significant resources, with the understanding that you will implement a punitive fee for certain food products we deem unfit for the public health. A penny-per-ounce tax could reduce consumption of sugared beverages by more than 10 percent, while adding substantial revenue to the city coffers."

"Higher taxes don't typically sit well with the public. How am I supposed to sell that?"

"You don't, silly," smiled the woman, revealing tomato-red lipstick smeared on her teeth. "You keep it all hush-hush for the time being. Don't introduce the legislation until you've already been reelected."

Reverend Dave knew this to be the conventional strategy, but these days he was finding it harder and harder to keep such plans quiet. He suspected everyone working for the city of being a turncoat. The sugar strategy was tempting, but risky.

"I also have other friends in the dietary lobby with whom you may be interested in speaking. Like-minded people with big bank accounts."

The mayor's mouth was watering. "And who might they be?"

"Mayor Cornelius," she tapped her well-manicured nails on the table. "What do you know about trans-fat?"

***

"*Gooooooood morning, Birmingham!*" greeted Mad Marty Madigan over the airwaves. "They say that when you mess with the bull, you get the horns, and my guest today proves exactly that. I'd like to bring back a gentleman from Fulton Springs who says he's mad as hell and he's not gonna take it anymore! And after a harrowing incident at his place of business last Friday night, many people—many potential voters—are characterizing his anger as righteous indignation! Currently running for mayor of Fulton

Springs, please welcome Frank Standish, owner of The Bull barbecue restaurant, to the Marty Madigan Show ... Pleasure to see you, sir."

"Likewise," said Frank. The show's producer, Vanessa, had contacted Frank after seeing the incident covered on the nightly news.

"How's the campaign going? I've seen your opponent's campaign ads all over the telly, but I don't think I've seen yours."

"That's right, Mr. Madigan. At this time I don't have the same campaign finances as the current mayor. He's got money to burn because he sold out the Fulton Springs citizens to special interest groups."

"What kind of special interest groups?"

"As I reported last time, he recently unveiled a plan to restrict the use of salt in the city's restaurants. I run a barbecue joint, and he's screwing with my recipes. That means he's restricting my freedom, limiting my ability to run my business as I see fit—and doing the same to all the Fulton Springs restaurant owners. For that proposed legislation, he received a big check to pay for those TV ads. Guess what's next on the table? Restrictions on sugar and trans-fat. If the mayor gets his way, we'll all be eating rice cakes morning, noon and night. To the people of Fulton Springs, I say this: If you reelect the mayor, you're voting to restrict your own freedoms."

"I hear you loud and clear, Frank. Nanny-state government has got to go," said Madigan. "My grandfather has a saying: 'Every man deserves to go to hell in his own fashion.' I've always agreed with that. Give me another example of these special interest groups."

"The mayor also grants city contracts only to his friends—and by that I mean supporters—through a no-bid process. So the taxpaying citizens of Fulton Springs are paying top dollar for his buddies' sweetheart deals. And you don't get cozy with the mayor unless you contribute to his campaign. See a pattern? The average

Fulton Springs contractor doesn't get to benefit from an open-bid process for the jobs that are funded by their very own tax dollars."

"Can you prove that?" asked Madigan.

"All due respect, I don't need to prove it to you, Marty. I live in a small community. These kind of shenanigans are common knowledge among the people of my town, and that's who I've got to wake up and convince to vote for me."

"According to the news, it sounds like one of the mayor's new laws put you and your wife in a dangerous predicament over the weekend," said Madigan. "You were injured. I understand if you're not comfortable with the topic, but would you care to elaborate?"

News of Frank Standish's stouthearted clash with two armed hooligans had covered Fulton Springs like springtime pollen. Likewise, word of his eagerly awaited first-hand account had captivated the community. The townsfolk made the morning's radio interview the social event of the week, gathering in garages and over kitchen counters to lean into their radios like a campfire on a cold night.

On mention of the burglary, Frank's demeanor darkened. "The mayor disarmed us. He made gun possession illegal, which I don't even think is constitutional. That jackass disarmed everyone in the city and let the crooks know that he was doing it. He put his citizens in jeopardy and made the city perfectly safe for criminals. No surprise that the criminals responded in kind. A group of them burglarized several establishments in the city last Friday, the very night that the new law was enforced. My business was one of the establishments. My wife was attacked by two armed men. We did not have our legally registered firearm to defend ourselves, and the police were nowhere to be seen. They failed to protect us. Only by the grace of God did my wife escape without serious injury."

"Hmmm," Madigan shook his head. "I'm truly glad to hear she was not seriously injured. From what I've been told, you showed up in the nick of time, and more or less lit into the burglars like a pit bull on a toddler."

Frank was embarrassed. "My wife was being attacked. I lost my temper."

"You took out two armed men. And I hear you gave 'em a real makeover."

"One is still in a coma," said Frank. "I didn't intend for that to happen." Although his blood would still boil at the very thought of the attack, Frank regretted hurting the thieves so severely.

Madigan laughed a bit awkwardly. "Words of remorse from a man who was defending his wife from attack. The reluctant hero, Frank Standish."

Fulton Springs residents were swapping high fives all over town. Triple-threat Frank Standish, the racing legend and barbecue mogul, was now a slayer of dragons. Compared to the dreary drabness of the bloated mayor, Frank was looking like a human muscle car, and the people wanted to hear him rev.

"The incident on Friday was the last straw," said Standish. "And, as I understand it, the burglars who invaded my business were the same thugs who mugged the mayor just a few days ago." That crucial bit of information, heretofore unreported, came directly from the Fulton Springs Police Department courtesy of Frank's anonymous source, Officer Art Brookings.

Madigan was speechless, momentarily oblivious of the empty airwaves. "The mayor was mugged? You caught the thieves? Are you kidding me?"

Frank's stony silence rendered the question rhetorical. Shane Painter had been found in possession of the mayor's phone, and T.B had his wallet.

Madigan pursed his lips and released a long whistle. "Wow," he said. "That's certainly an ironic twist of fate."

Frank lowered his head closer to the microphone. "Now I've got a direct challenge to our standing mayor." His expression was grave. Frank lifted a fist and choked the base of the receiver. He took a deep breath and glassed the room. Madigan and Vanessa were both staring at him intently. The young assistant serving coffee sensed the tension and stopped moving.

"I know the mayor's out there," said Frank, his voice like dragging a brick on asphalt. "I know he's probably listening right now." Frank cracked his knuckles.

The crew of the radio station was engrossed in the drama.

"I'm challenging Mayor Davenport Cornelius to a policy debate at Six Mile Park one week from Friday. If he wants to criticize me on TV, then maybe he'll have the guts to show up and do it face to face. Six o'clock sharp. I'll be there. I'd like to see him defend his new rules and regs like a man, not just a mouthpiece. At the very least, I think he owes that to the people of Fulton Springs."

For a moment Mad Marty Madigan expected a tumbleweed to bounce through the station. He thought he heard the distant cry of a buzzard.

"Wow," said Madigan into his mic. "You heard it here first, folks. Frank Standish, the self-described one-term candidate, throwing down the gauntlet for the incumbent mayor of Fulton Springs. This race is really heating up. We'll be back after this break."

***

Derek walked out of the chicken stand with his lunch of buffalo strips and French fries. He was planning to swallow it on the way to visit Grandma Standish, a Saturday afternoon tradition, but as he settled in his Mustang and shifted into reverse, he saw in the rearview mirror that he was blocked by a Fulton Springs police cruiser. The cruiser chirped its siren as a signal to halt. Derek shifted back into park, perplexed.

Officer Farling approached the window and tapped it with his Maglite, motioning to Derek to roll it down.

Derek begrudgingly obliged with a sinking feeling.

"Afternoon, Standish," greeted Farling disdainfully.

"Officer," nodded Derek.

"How we doing today?" Farling asked from behind his mirrored sunglasses.

"Peachy," said Derek. "Is there some sort of problem?"

Farling smiled for a moment and then released a long, dramatic sigh. "Well ... I hope not son, I really do." He shook his head ruefully. "The thing is, we've had a shoplifting incident at the Chevron station up the road. The clerk gave us a description of the culprit and, shockingly, you fit that description."

Derek was wearing blue jeans and a blank white undershirt.

"Are you serious? Half the guys in this town are wearing jeans and a t-shirt."

"Mmm-hmmm," said Farling, turning away dismissively. "I'm going to have to ask you to step out of the car."

Derek obeyed, seeing no other option. Farling asked Derek to wait with his stone-faced partner beside the cruiser as Farling circled the car, looking through the windows.

"Do I have permission to search your vehicle?" asked Farling.

"No. I do not give you permission to search my vehicle," Derek emphasized each word to be completely clear. "I haven't done anything wrong."

"You realize that I have probable cause, right? You fit the description of a robbery suspect." Farling opened the door and bent to check beneath the seat.

Derek knew it was useless to protest.

"Besides, in the State of Alabama we have something called the Wingspan Law." He kneeled into the driver's seat to rummage through the rest of the car. "Do you know what that is? The wingspan law says I may legally search the suspect's immediate area—in other words, your 'wingspan'—without a search warrant. This is so the suspect cannot reach for a weapon or destroy evidence. It just so happens that since I stopped the suspect inside his car, the entire interior of the vehicle could be considered within the suspect's 'wingspan.' That sort of determination is generally left to the discretion of the arresting officer. Know what I mean, son?"

Derek knew what it meant: that cops had the power to stick it in and break it off whenever they wanted; so much for privacy or property rights. Derek was in a thorny situation. He was on probation, and Farling knew it. If Derek was caught committing any infraction, he would have to return to Judge Roper for a reevaluation of his sentence, which reportedly was never a good thing.

Thankfully, Derek was out of sign-making materials. His highway banners were a fresh irritation to the local police and would have provided Farling a fresh, new charge.

Regretfully, the banners were not the only contraband Derek had to worry about.

"Well, well, well," said the cop as he backed his wide rear end out of the Mustang, dangling a plastic baggie from his fingertips like a dirty diaper. "Look what I found under the passenger seat, Hobson!" he shouted to his partner. "Looks like we got us a regular Willie Nelson."

The wooden-faced officer turned to Derek. "You been smoking the ganja, Standish?"

Officer Farling shoved the bag of marijuana at Derek's face. "Looks like you're in a heap of trouble, son. I had a feeling that you'd be passing through my jail again."

Derek knew he was toast. Farling was going to book him for anything and everything he could, and there was nothing Derek could do to discourage him. It was about a vendetta.

"How's your son's face healing?" asked Derek. He had left Farling's son a token of remembrance—a dent-like scar on the side of his forehead.

Farling's hateful gaze pierced Derek's eyes, burned through his brain and bored out the back of his head. The officer bit down hard and ground his teeth. He wanted so badly to punch this punk in the head, to smash his smirking little face. Instead, he would throw him in jail after a humiliating strip search.

"Never speak about my son again," growled Farling. He cut his eyes at Hobson and said, "Throw this turd in the backseat. Let's drive him up to the Chevron and see if the clerk can I.D. him. We'll see what other crimes he's committed."

Derek's carton of spicy chicken fingers was abandoned on the trunk of his car, going stale in the afternoon air.

***

Despite the mayor's ubiquitous televised attack ads, Frank's campaign seemed to have developed a life of its own. On his way to The Bull, Frank noticed that supportive campaign signs were appearing on lawns throughout the city. Some of them were signs Fancy and Sharon had ordered from a print shop, but as soon as they were posted in public places, the police pulled them up and disposed of them on orders from the mayor. However, the authorities were powerless to snuff the signs on private property, and they popped up like weeds after a summer rain. Most of the signs were homemade, demonstrating the genuine grassroots activism his campaign had inspired. People were painting their own plywood sandwich boards and artfully decorating them with personalized slogans.

"One Term Will Keep 'Em Honest—Frank Standish for Mayor."

"Take back Six Mile Creek—Vote Standish."

"Don't let an obese man tell you what to eat! Vote Standish for mayor."

Private citizens were getting away with the kind of rhetoric that would sink a politician. Lawns were just the beginning. Homemade bumper stickers and rear-windshield signs were cropping up like a record harvest.

"Tired of lining their pockets? Vote Standish."

"Vote for freedom. Vote for Standish."

"RESIST CONTROL—Standish for mayor!"

For the first time, Frank felt as though the wind was at his back and his efforts had gained some momentum. People were excited, and electricity was in the air. Frank realized that some of the homes posting signs of support were long-term parishioners of Reverend Dave's church. The mayor's nanny-state overtures to drum up financial support for his election were alienating his base with fantastic irony.

***

The cold metal bars, harsh lighting and stale air of his jail cell made Derek feel like a lab specimen awaiting the next round of some experimental treatment. He was isolated in a cell away from the general population of inmates, which he supposed was intended as extra punishment from Officer Farling even though he actually preferred the solitude.

Being his second stint in the slammer, he was much cooler and more collected than on his first visit, when he had been paralyzed with fear. His last was a truly harrowing experience, as Derek was unaccustomed to the legal machinations of being arrested and deeply feared he would be stuck in jail for some grueling eternity. This time he was confident his grandmother—recipient of his "one phone call"—would soon arrive to post bail. He knew he was in trouble, but he also knew it was a relatively minor offense in a world of murders and rapes, and that his punishment would not be meted out immediately. Although a court date would darken the days ahead and a lawyer's retainer would surely flat-line his savings, at least by nightfall he would be comfortably back at home, wishing ill will on the Farlings of the world from the warmth and safety of his bed sheets.

"You posted bail," said the jailer as he jingled the keys into the cell door. He swung it open with a squeak and motioned Derek toward the front wing of the police station.

After collecting his personal effects, he was lead to the front desk where his grandmother stood with an expression of embarrassed contrition. It pained him to see that look on her face.

His explanation to the desk clerk that he was already enjoying a close relationship with a parole officer and did not need a new one was met with a scolding glare. He then collected his court-date notice and signed his release papers. As he stepped into the parking lot, he drew a vigorous breath of fresh air and freedom.

"Son, I am so very sorry you had to go through that unfortunate business," said Edna Standish.

"Grandma, please. Don't apologize for anything. For crying out loud, I was arrested for possessing an illegal plant. Just saying it out loud sounds ridiculous. It's a stupid law and I don't regret anything I've done."

She still looked hurt. "But it's going to cause trouble for you, baby. Whether you agree with it or not, it's the law."

"I know it's the law. But it's not right. There's a gulf of difference between what's right and wrong, and what's legal and illegal."

She smiled weakly as she drove the car down Main Street. Derek placed his hand on her knee and squeezed to reassure her. He knew the last thing she needed was to worry about his welfare. She had her own health to consider.

***

Back at The Bull, the news of Derek's arrest hit Frank like a thrown brick. He was fuming. Frank felt like a wash rag twisted to wring out the water, unable to wrap his mind around the idea that his son could do something so stupid. He was rushing through the dishes while playing out the arrest scenario in his mind, unconsciously slamming the glassware from sink to sink with a clattering racket, sloshing about a sudsy mess. The kitchen was in chaos, and when he slung one of the beer mugs into the rinser, it caught the edge of the stainless counter and shattered everywhere.

"DAMMIT!" boomed Frank, hurling the mug's glass handle against a tile wall where it, too, burst into pieces. He knelt down and brought his hand to his brow, noticing that the wound on his calf was bleeding again. That's how Fancy found him when she walked into the kitchen.

"Everything okay?" she asked, knowing the answer after hearing the racket.

Frank said nothing, so she approached him and hooked an arm over his shoulders. She ran her long nails through his hair, and the gesture had an instant, almost magical, calming effect on him. She kissed his forehead and knelt silently beside him, understanding. It was exactly what Frank's frayed nerves needed.

"He's a good kid, you know." smiled Fancy.

Frank just kept glowering at the floor.

"He may have made a mistake," she consoled, "but he's still a good kid. You need to remember that before you confront him. And you need to calm down, too."

"I didn't raise my kid to be some sort of dope fiend," he grumbled.

Fancy rolled her eyes. "Frank Standish, you old codger ..."

125

Frank lifted his head and raised an eyebrow.

She met him with a knowing look. "You know good and well that Derek's not some 'dope fiend'. Let's not forget that you were no angel when you were his age."

"I was stupid."

"You were young. You took risks. Some of them were not very smart. And as I recall, you had your own run-ins with the law."

"I grew out of it. And I didn't want him to grow into it. He's got too much to lose. Back in my day, the cops would usually just dump the grass on the road and chase us home. These days, that kind of trouble can follow a guy around, screw up future job opportunities. He's got too much to lose to be screwing up like this."

She rubbed his shoulders and turned his face up to meet her own. "Have you talked to your son, yet?"

His eyes fell away.

"No," she answered for him. "You haven't even talked to him. Here you are judging him without giving him a day in court."

He said nothing

"Look at me ..." she said, lifting his head with her hands. He obeyed. "Here's some tried and true parenting advice: Go talk to your son." Fancy kissed his forehead, stood and walked away.

***

Pierce took a long pull from the joint and then passed it to Billy Farling with a roll of the fingers. Mission accomplished, he thought. The arrest of Derek Standish was executed as if scripted. He had known for months that he and Standish shared a common illicit acquaintance, and it only took a hundred dollars for Pierce to convince their mutual marijuana dealer to keep him appraised of Derek's buying habits.

It was Billy, eager for vengeance, who had served as the conduit of this information to his father, the police chief. The elder Farling, who detested the Standish clan as much as his son did, was so eager to put a boot on their necks that he never pressed with questions about how Billy came across such criminal information. All Officer Farling cared to know was when and where Derek would be with the contraband.

Pierce had actually followed Derek's car at a distance as he left the dealer the morning of the arrest, relating his whereabouts by cell phone to Billy who tipped the information to his father. Once the cops had the coordinates—The Henhouse Chicken Shack—Pierce drove away and let the officers do their work. It was a thing of beauty.

"It's a shame that Standish asshole was involved in such shady activities," said Billy, giggling.

"Yes, it is," said Pierce. "Now pass me that doobie."

***

Frank took Fancy's advice insofar as speaking with his son, but as someone often emotionally distant and poorly communicative with his family, he failed to handle the matter with the delicate diplomacy she had suggested.

"What the hell were you thinking?" he asked Derek.

Startled, Derek's heart skipped a beat. He had slipped into the kitchen to snag some midnight cookies from the cupboard. He had not seen his father sitting in the shadows.

"Give me a break, Dad," replied his son wearily. "It's been a long week."

Frank slammed his coffee mug on the kitchen counter. "I want to know what's wrong with you! You're smarter than this!"

Derek raised his hands, one holding an Oatmeal Creme Pie. "Smarter than what?"

"Than wasting your time and your mind on dope!"

"Don't give me that. You own a bar. You sell alcohol. It's hypocritical."

Frank's face flushed a shade red. "I own a restaurant. And what I do is legal."

"Not after midnight," said Derek. "Not on Sunday mornings. And if some prohibition lobby flashes money at the mayor, maybe it won't be legal at all."

"You've got too much to lose to mess around with drugs."

"Those slot machines you had? Illegal. The smoking section in your restaurant? Illegal. You don't seem to care what's legal or not. You're making a moral judgment, and it's hypocritical. "

His son's arrest had immolated him with a sense of moral superiority, which had not prepared him for Derek's combative attitude. Frank's fury was brimming; he was an axe ready to fall. "Son, I'd advise you not to call me a hypocrite again."

Derek said nothing, only hung his head, steaming.

"You're on parole, for cryin' out loud!" said Frank.

"On parole for standing up for myself! For following your advice! How fair is that?"

Frank shook his head. "'Stand up for yourself' does not mean 'brain somebody with a hunk of metal!'"

Derek met Frank's steely gaze. "Yeah? Well, it worked."

Frank saw Derek's stubbornness as a reflection of his own. It was aggravating.

"Son, I'm gonna lay it down where the goats can get it," he said in a low growl, trying not to shout. "This issue is not open for debate. You are a grown adult capable of making your own decisions—I recognize that. But you're still living in my basement, under my roof, and your decisions have consequences. No matter what your personal views on marijuana are, the fact is that it's illegal. The criminal consequences of possessing it can ruin your life, whether you agree politically with that stark reality or not. And I'm not going to sit idly by while you live under my roof and watch you flush your life away. So as long as you continue to reside on my property, you'll follow my rules. And I forbid the possession of illegal drugs ... *Forbid it!* It's a deal-breaker. You got it?"

Derek let out an exasperated sigh. Frank grabbed him sternly by the arm. *"You got it!"* he roared.

"Yeah," said Derek, shaken. "I got it." He wrenched his arm away from his father.

"Good!" yelled Frank. "Then stay out of trouble!"

Derek grabbed his leather jacket and stormed out of the room.

Frank's eyes followed his son down the hall, his body rocking with rage. Somewhere in the back of his mind, he knew he had not handled the situation as deftly as he should have. For some reason that he could not recognize, he was more comfortable expressing anger to his son than appreciation. It was a truth, a failure, that he could not quite explain but deeply regretted. And the resulting animosity between him and his son: He hated it.

***

Fulton Springs was on fire with excitement over the big showdown to which Frank had challenged the mayor, just three days away. Everyone was volleying the burning question: Would Cornelius meet his opponent face to face, or remain skulking in the background, deriding Standish only from the safety of TV? Speculation was rampant but the court of public opinion seemed to agree on one crucial point: If the mayor did not show up, the mayor would look like a coward.

Frank was dealing out dishes left and right during the lunchtime rush. As soon as Rocky had the food ready, Frank was acrobatically slinging the rib plates and brisket sandwiches to his wait-staff for the hordes of supporters who were visiting his restaurant from open to close over the past several days. His candidacy was evolving into a modest cultural phenomenon that he would never have imagined just mere months ago.

During the frenzy of his food prep, Frank noticed from the corner of his eye that a crowd was gathering on the front sidewalk. Some of the diners were leaving their seats to step outside and see what was so interesting. Oddly, they seemed to be looking upward.

Nathan Stevenson approached the bar excitedly, pointing skyward with both hands. "Frank, come outside for a second!" he said, "I think this is something you're gonna want to see."

The food was coming fast, and Nathan volunteered to relieve Frank while he took a break. Curiosity brimming, Frank wiped his hands and limped his way through the crowd, people beaming at him and patting him on the back. As he pushed the door open, he heard a distant engine. It was not an automobile or one of the city lawnmowers. It was the distinct timbre of an airplane, and Frank shaded his eyes and peered upward.

"Where in the world did that come from?" asked Frank.

"That is Fred Matthews," said Sharon McClendon who had stopped by for a salad. "I heard he was going to do this, but we all wanted to surprise you."

"Who's that?" said Frank.

"You met him when you were petitioning for signatures. I guess you made an impression. He felt like you were getting the shaft with the mayor's TV commercials, so he wanted to level the playing field as best he could."

A small airplane was circling the city with a long banner rippling in tow. The banner stated in big block text: VOTE STANDISH THE ONE TERM MAYOR.

Frank stared upward in awe. The gesture was swelling a huge lump in his throat.

"Fred is retired now, but his sons still run his aerial advertising service down on the gulf coast. So he called in some favors. He believes in you Frank," said Sharon, patting him on the back. "We all do."

Frank choked back the lump, but dared not turn from the sky for a moment lest a tear roll from his eye. He choked them back as well. Then he nodded, lowered his head and said, "That's real nice of him," with a shaky smile.

Frank returned to the kitchen to distract himself with work, grinding away at his swelling emotions with a mental mortar and pestle. But as he did, the crowd broke into spontaneous applause. And the applause became cheers. And the cheers became chants. *"One-term mayor! One-term mayor! One-term mayor!"*

That was the moment Frank realized he was no longer in control of the campaign. He was just along for the ride.

***

Evidence of his teetering support had led Mayor Cornelius to develop a new habit—calming his nerves with a plug of whiskey in his morning coffee. And his mid-morning coffee. Followed by a cocktail at lunch. He hid the indulgence from his colleagues to maintain a professional appearance, but the rank smell of liquor belying his cheap cologne tipped the truth to everyone in city hall. The mayor's tires were showing the wire, and people were noticing.

"Standish has us cornered, sir," said Pierce to the mayor, who sat across from his big mahogany desk. "We're in a precarious situation."

The mayor ran his tongue around the upturned cup for the last drops of his special mid-morning brew. He withdrew the cup and said, "Nonsense. We own the airwaves, and he's a small-timer."

The mayor was as unconvincing as he was unconvinced. Piece recognized it as denial, and was concerned Cornelius was resigned to merely go through the motions of the campaign, riding on blind faith, rather than plotting a proactive strategy to stem the tide of his challenger's support. Standish's momentum was evidenced by the countless banners, billboards, bumper stickers and homemade yard signs that peppered virtually every neighborhood in town.

Pierce had organized a team of college interns—kids he did not have to pay—to mount a response to Frank's grassroots success. The interns were dispatched throughout the city, posting hundreds of Cornelius campaign signs in the high-traffic areas of the public right-of-way. The mayor's signs were under no threat of removal by the police.

"We have the Lord on our side," said the mayor. "Nothing to fear." He hiccupped.

"When you don't show up for the debate, you'll look to the public like you've got a lot to fear," said Pierce.

The mayor leaned back in his large leather chair and crumpled the coffee cup.

"There won't be any debate," said the mayor. "Standish forgot who the hell runs this town. He's been denied a permit to assemble. And I'll have Farling and some other officers blocking the gates with cruisers to prevent any park access, in case he thinks he's above the law. With no debate, I still control the conversation with the TV exposure. Done and done."

Pierce slumped in his chair. "Standish has stirred up a lot of excitement about this thing. People want to see you go head to head. They want to see sparks fly. You can't just shut him down and expect to win by default. You'll look like the kid who didn't show up for the after-school fight."

"Well, I'm not showing up. Showing up will look like I'm kowtowing to his demands, and he doesn't get to make demands."

"I'm not saying you should show up," said Pierce, who had no doubt that in an honest debate, Standish would beat the mayor like a bad dog. "But you have to respond to the challenge. Sir, with all due respect, if you snuff his debate without a response, they'll say you're running with your tail between your legs. You've got to respond. You've got make the next move, but you've got to do it on your own terms."

Cornelius ruffled at the thought of appearing cowardly. He pulled a handkerchief from his breast pocket and blotted his forehead. "What do you propose?"

Pierce sat back up in his chair and cleared his throat. "We don't have much ammo left," he said. "But Farling popped Standish's son on a drug charge. That could be our ace. The son still lives with Standish. It looks like he doesn't have his own house in order. How can he be expected to govern the town?" He held up his hands.

"What kind of drug charge?"

"Just a pot charge," said Mathers. "Still, this ain't Colorado. It's plenty enough to stir up the blue-hairs at your church. The son broke the law. It calls into question the Standish family's moral character and the father's capacity to lead. We need to double down on the moral character issue. You're a preacher. You have some credibility on those kind of matters."

"But we only have a few days."

"That's why you're going back into the TV studio today. Get ready to spend some money. You're going to have to empty the clip. We've got to saturate the TV with commercials. Radio, too. So sober up."

The mayor chafed at the suggestion of drunkenness, but Pierce held up a hand that told him to save it.

"You will not respond to his criticisms in the commercial. You're above that. You'll not respond to the man's concerns over taxes, guns or food regulation. You will steer the conversation to the sinful nature of the Standish family. Lay it on thick, Reverend. You have to scare the people. They've got to learn that he represents a great evil that will infect the rest of the city if he's elected."

The mayor knew his options were limited. He leaned back, folded his hands behind his head and contemplated this final salvo. "Fine," he said. "Let's do this."

***

The Bull was packed from wall to wall when the mayor's new commercial premiered during the five o'clock local news.

The televisions boomed with a clap of thunder, and stock footage of a stormy horizon illuminated the screen.

"First, he brought the booze," warned the narrator with cryptic urgency. The sight of an overturned can of malt liquor faded into view.

"Then, he brought the gambling." The strident ringing of a busy casino backed stock footage of a craps table in action.

"Now, here come the drugs!" Handcuffs were clamped behind the back of an unidentified man, and then the scene dissolved to a jail cell as its barred door slammed shut.

"Frank Standish's own son was recently arrested on a charge of possessing marijuana. Frank Standish is running for mayor of Fulton Springs. If Frank Standish can't maintain a virtuous household, how can he be trusted to maintain a virtuous city?"

Reverend Dave appeared on screen with a Bible before him. "Hello, I'm Davenport Cornelius, mayor of Fulton Springs. For the past seven years I've governed our city with a single guiding principle—to provide a quiet, wholesome and pleasant place to raise a family. But I now fear that our Godly way of life is being threatened. Frank Standish simply does not exhibit the moral character we expect from our city officials. His earthly pursuits simply do not square with the traditional values of the Fulton Springs citizens, and now we're learning that the evils of drugs have infected his family. His candidacy threatens to pull this town into the slums of iniquity, and I need your help to keep our city a nice, safe place to live. Please, vote

Davenport Cornelius for mayor. Thanks for your support, and God bless Fulton Springs."

When the TV spot was over, The Bull was silent except for the abrasive jingle of the next commercial.

***

The night before the debate, Frank was trying on his favorite button-up shirt when Fancy came in carrying a new suit for him. She hung it on the door and then spread a beach towel on the floor. Then Sharon McClendon entered the room and placed a folding chair on the towel. Frank had not expected to see Sharon in his home. Fancy scooped him around the waist as part of a carefully coordinated ambush. She landed him in the metal chair, and Sharon, a hair stylist by trade, tied an apron around his neck. When Sharon descended with the scissors, Frank took evasive action.

"Wait just a minute. What's going on?" He had been in a miserable mood ever since the latest round of TV ads launched the assault on his family's reputation.

"I decided you need a little work," said Fancy. "I asked Sharon to help. I love you, but you're scruffy looking. You have to be presentable to the public."

"I'm already beautiful," grumbled Frank.

"Of course you are, Sweetie," said Sharon, "but your wife's right. You could use a little touching up."

"A lot of politics boils down to image," said Fancy. "We need to overhaul yours for public consumption."

"You haven't had a problem with me before now."

"And I don't have a problem with you now," she said. "But let's face it, you're kind of a sourpuss and you dress like a redneck."

Sharon giggled.

Frank's hands went into the air. "That's who I am! I'm not changing who I am."

"Frank Standish, behave like a grown-up!" teased Sharon while brushing his hair.

"Nobody's trying to change who you are," said Fancy. "However, if you're going to kiss babies and shake hands, then you need a haircut and a shave. Otherwise you'll scare people, sweetheart."

Frank opened his mouth to protest and Fancy put her finger over his lips, kneeling down to meet him at eye level. "This is happening," she whispered.

He knew it was pointless to resist. He capitulated, pouting throughout the haircut.

Fancy knew that deep down Frank loved the attention.

"The next thing we're going to work on is your smile," said Fancy.

"My what?"

"Your face, silly. You frown too much. If you want to win votes, then you need to show those pearly whites. Who wants to vote for a grumpy old man?"

The rest of the evening Fancy coached Frank on his smile, which he practiced in the mirror like an idiot.

Whether Frank would admit it or not, Fancy knew she had lifted his spirits. Her plan was a secret success.

***

On Friday afternoon, a crisp autumn breeze gave the air a slight chill, but the sky was clear and blue. Any southern football fan was apt to describe it as perfect game-day weather, and the people of Fulton Springs were eager for kickoff.

The Standish campaign had settled on six o'clock to start the Great Debate, although none of his supporters believed the mayor would actually show up. The city's denial of Frank's permit to assemble had plainly stated the reverend's intent. His Highness would use the event's illegality—a status which he bestowed upon it—to excuse his absence from the public challenge.

Rev. Dave's actions came as no surprise, and Frank's campaign proceeded, completely undeterred, as though a permit were not a legal requirement. Frank was counting on the mayor's evasion to speak volumes about the man's character. If the mayor could not muster the courage to meet his challenger face to face to level the same allegations he lobbed from afar in his TV ads, then his attacks would appear at best questionable, perhaps baseless, and at worst wholly fabricated for the sole purpose of sealing his reelection bid. At least, that was Frank's hope. Integrity was still a vaunted virtue in the South. If one man could not look another in the eye when calling him a snake, then that one man appeared to have something to hide—and the other man looked less like a snake. Maybe enough voters would pay attention.

Since everyone who supported Frank expected the mayor to hide like a dog from thunder, they resolved to use the occasion as a final rally to generate enthusiasm on the eve of the big election.

They did not, however, expect to encounter the wholesale shutdown of the public park.

At 5:45 Frank and Fancy turned the corner entering the park. They were met by dozens of cars idling bumper-to-bumper, with droves more accumulating behind Frank's truck with every passing second.

He saw the flash of police lights ahead. Ahead of the cars were rows of traffic cones and orange and white sawhorses. Two police cruisers were parked across both lanes of traffic, orbiting a lolling blue flash over the roadway.

"Looks like we've got a problem." Frank shifted to park and unbuckled his seat belt. As he cracked open the door an officer approached, and Frank could tell by his dragging gait and the way his head was hung that it must be Art Brookings.

"Howdy, Frank," said Brookings, lifting his face with a pained expression. "You know I hate being put in these situations, right?"

Frank lit a cigarette. "What *is* the situation, Art?

Brookings released a long, weary sigh. "I'm sorry about this. I really am. If I'd known sooner that the mayor was going to pull this crap, I would've sent word."

"The mayor closed the park?"

At that moment, Derek's Mustang rumbled up beside Frank's truck on the shoulder. Frank turned to his son, recognizing the growl of the engine. Frank used to own the car, rebuilt it with his son and then gave him the title as a high-school graduation present. They held each other's glance for a moment. Derek gave his dad a single, curt nod of the head. Frank returned the gesture. That was the extent of their reconciliation.

"The mayor knew you'd show up tonight. Permit or not. You're predictable that way," smiled Art.

"Just out of curiosity," Frank asked, "what reason did he give for closing the park? It's never been closed before. What was his ...

justification?"

Brookings shrugged. "Justification? Hell, I was just told to close it down and run everybody off. I wasn't given a reason, Frank. That's not the way the good reverend works."

Across the park, Frank could see that its northern entrance was also barricaded. The police on that end were motioning drivers to turn around, explaining no event was to be allowed and that everyone should just go home. It appeared that six police vehicles and at least eight officers had been dispatched to this assignment.

"Oh my goodness, look at that little cutie!" Fancy suddenly said from the passenger's seat.

She hopped out of the truck and gathered a silver cat that had appeared on the hood, seemingly out of nowhere. She climbed back into the truck with the feline in her arms. "Do you remember this cat?" asked Fancy. "He hangs around the restaurant. I think I'm going to keep him."

Frank looked at the cat. The cat looked back. Its eyes twinkled knowingly, and it meowed at Frank. Fancy's impulsiveness was among his wife's many charms, and as unenthusiastic as he was about adopting a new animal, he knew perfectly well they had already done that the second Fancy scooped up the cat. Besides, although he could not get his mind around exactly what his gut told him, he felt there was something wise about that cat.

"Let's go, Brookings!" shouted Officer Farling from the front of the traffic jam. "We got cars stacking up! Clear 'em out! We ain't got all day!"

Brookings fumed. "That guy rubs me like 80-grit toilet paper."

"It looks like most of your shift is assigned to this one location," said Frank.

Brookings glassed the park. "Yeah, it is," he said. "It'd be a crying shame if we had all our eggs in this one basket, while somebody held some sort of event in a totally different place. We'd be spread a little thin to do much about it."

"I see," said Frank, shifting the truck into drive. "Then I guess we'd better vacate the premises."

"One minute," said Art, raising a finger and jogging to the trunk of his cruiser. He returned with a large cardboard box, which he dropped in the bed of Frank's truck.

"That's a campaign donation from the Fulton Springs Police Department, whether that fat jackass in charge likes it or not." Art flashed a big grin.

Frank gave him a military salute. "Thank you for your support."

As Frank curled the truck onto the shoulder in a U-turn, Derek followed in his Mustang. The noise of blaring car horns filled the air, and the drivers of the idling vehicles began booing and shouting at the police.

"What now?" asked Fancy. "I know you aren't packing up and going home."

Frank thought for a moment. In his rearview mirror he saw his son following. Then another car pulled behind the Mustang. Then another. A spontaneous caravan was emerging from the park.

"I'm going to The Bull, baby," he said. "Where else?" He had no plan but figured he would at least regroup.

An electronic chime chirped from Fancy's purse, and she pulled out her cellular phone.

"Hey, honey" she answered. She listened intently, leaning her head into the phone and nodding with the conversation. Frank grew curious. "Sounds good to me," she said. "Certainly worth a try … Okay, let's give it a shot."

Fancy folded the phone and tucked it back inside her purse.

"Who was that?" asked Frank, steering the truck onto the highway, with the long procession of vehicles tailing behind him.

"That was your son," she said. "He had an idea for you."

"An idea? What idea?"

"Frank, have you ever heard of a flash mob?"

***

Barry Finkelstein was hanging upside-down from a tree, harnessing the last rays of the setting sun with a magnifying glass to incinerate a line of army ants. His phone rang with the tune of "Way Down South in Dixie."

He pulled it from his pocket. "Finkelstein Electrical," he greeted. *"We've got spark!"*

"Barry! Where are you?" Derek asked.

"In a tree, burning ants."

"You're supposed to be at the rally!"

"Oh crap! That's today?"

As he made a mad dash to his car, Barry began phoning everyone he knew.

***

"Hey, Momma Cooper! How you doin'?" said Rocky into the phone. Rock kept Mabel Cooper updated on the latest news about the city election. With her restaurant's vested interest in the new dietary regulations, she had given her entire kitchen staff a paid night off to support Frank at the rally.

"We're doing fine, honey, but the police up here at the park told us to go home. We got six car loads full of my workers. Where we supposed to go?"

"Momma, don't you worry. Round up your crew and send 'em over to The Bull. We ain't throwin' in the towel yet."

***

"Hello?" said Frieda Collins. "Hello!" Frieda shook her cell phone angrily. "HELLO! *HELLO!* ... Speak up! I can't understand what you're saying!"

"You should give me the phone, Frieda," came a voice from the front of the car. "You're hard of hearing."

"Stuff it, Selby!" she shouted to her driver.

"Why are all the cars leaving?" asked Betsy Willingham, who shared the back of the Cadillac with Frieda. They were stuck in the Six Mile traffic, and the car was a bevy of confusion.

"Why are the cars leaving?" screeched Frieda into the phone. "We were on the way to the park, but now all the cars are going the wrong way!"

***

"Mad" Marty Madigan and his producer, Vanessa, were among the cars expelled from Six Mile Park. They had arranged to supply the Standish campaign with a P.A. system and to cover the debate live on the radio via remote broadcast. The forced cancellation was rendering their effort a huge waste of time, and saddled them with a gaping hole in their programming schedule. Marty badly wanted a drink.

"Madigan here. What's up?" he said into the cell phone on its first ring.

Derek explained the situation.

"Where's The Bull?" asked Marty, nodding into the phone. "I see. And they have beer on tap?" He gave a thumbs-up to Vanessa. "Okay, I'm there."

***

Edna Standish had reluctantly decided not to attend the debate. Although she fully backed Frank's campaign, she had felt weak and nauseous all day and did not feel up to the commotion. But when Lilly Hathaway from her church prayer circle phoned to say Cornelius had not only refused to show up, but had completely closed the park and turned away the town, Edna got angry. She never did like a bully. Edna used that anger to climb out of bed, wrap a scarf around her head and snatch up the car keys to go show her support for her son.

***

Edna called three more friends. Mad Marty Madigan called his friend Daphne Shields. Derek sent instant messages to all 1,374 subscribers to the electronic newsletter he had started in support of his dad's campaign. Fulton Springs became a hotbed of unseen electronic activism, with phones ringing, text messages chiming, emails arriving, social sites buzzing, and in some cases, good old-fashioned word of mouth. The plans to regroup at The Bull for the final Standish rally spread through phone lines and satellite networks with an irrepressible invisible energy, throwing into motion a town full of people who did not like being told they could not gather at the town park that had been built with their taxes. They viewed the mayor's obstinance as unfounded, pernicious and tyrannical. His strong-arm methods were emblematic of everything Standish stood against, and it came at a time when a lot of fed-up people were ready to raise voice against exactly that type of authoritative repression.

Frank and Fancy had stopped to gas up and grab a beverage at the Quik Stop. By the time they reached Main Street, cars and trucks were convening around The Bull from every direction. Frank was amazed when he rounded the corner to the bar. Every parking space in sight was packed like a peanut can. The roads were jammed bumper to bumper. The shoulders were covered with parked vehicles, and the lawns were becoming invisible. A few of The Bull's regulars kept open a single lane that led Frank right to the front of The Bull. People were everywhere, and many were waving homemade signs. Some were familiar faces, but many he had never seen.

He pulled the truck slowly up the hill, mindful of the people, old and young alike, who mobbed the Main Street intersection to hear his ideas for the future of the city.

Fancy leaned over and placed her hand beneath Frank's open mouth. She pushed it close. "Don't catch a fly," she smiled.

Frank realized the turnout at The Bull far exceeded the traffic at the park. Although Frank had his loyal base, the mayor's latest round of televised character attacks had been effective at dampening the enthusiasm he had amassed from new supporters. In fact, Frank's erstwhile confidence had been secretly besieged with a sodden sense of doubt. Frank had anticipated a decent crowd at the park, but not the teeming masses that showed up at The Bull. Something had happened between there and here, in what seemed like just a few short moments, and Frank suspected he was witnessing the voter backlash that he had long hoped to see.

Flash mob, Fancy had said. When the mayor tried to silence the challenge to his authority, to crush the one-on-one debate, the town finally took notice—apparently—and did so with astonishing speed. Frank realized he was seeing the results of modern technology in action. He was not attune to the latest communicative gadgetry and networking applications, but he was also not naive. He owned a cell phone, and had been tutored in the art of texting by his daughter Nora. The phone was a "gift" from his wife, an item that often felt like an electronic leash but which he agreed to carry at Fancy's behest. He generally found little interest in the information age, but the spectacle before him was forcing Frank to reassess the power of interconnectivity.

The growing masses were a stunning testament to the fact that people in the South did not like being told to shut up. The mayor had tried to do exactly that. News of the reverend's move lit a fuse from person to person and house to house, spurred and spread through a pervasive system of modern data-transfer where all the latest news, every knee-jerk opinion, every happy thought or heated fit of rage could be communicated in real time and with real effect.

There had been an official decree: The mayor ran the show, and everyone else should shut the hell up and obey. It was enough to make a lot of Fulton Springs fence-sitters give pause even to a drinking, gambling, drugging bar owner who had a beef with the man in charge. After all, everyone deserved a day in court, and after the onslaught of TV commercials—which grated on the voters with their incessant negativity—Frank was at risk of being sentenced by public opinion, and that conflicted with many voters' sense of fair play.

Frank leaned over and hugged his wife. He then gave the silver cat a pat on the head.

"Today's your day to shine," Fancy told him.

"I'm glad you're in my corner," he said to them both. "I couldn't have done it without you." He kissed Fancy and stepped out of the truck.

The crowd around The Bull greeted him with cheers.

***

Sharon McClendon and Nathan Stevenson approached Frank from the front step. Nathan pantomimed a vaudevillian tip of the hat. "Your public awaits," he said, bowing dramatically.

Frank shook his head modestly. He leaned on the cane he had adopted while recovering from the stabbing, and Nathan and Sharon ushered him into the building as if they were leading a wounded heavyweight into the squared circle.

Back at Frank's truck, Derek appeared in the window and

kissed his stepmom on the cheek.

"This is really happening," said Derek, astounded at the turnout.

"It really is," she smiled.

Derek noticed the package in the truck bed. "What's in the box?"

Fancy peered through the rear windshield. "I don't know. A gift, I think, from Officer Brookings."

Derek leaned over the sidewall and broke open the lid. Neatly folded, carefully stacked, were the confiscated banners he had mounted over the interstate during the last several months. His heart lifted. A gift from a cop, he thought. The Lord did indeed work in mysterious ways.

"While Dad's getting ready, I've got some decorating to do. See you later, Mom." He kissed her cheek and disappeared into the crowd.

Derek weaved through the crowd with the big box and met with Opie and the Ortiz brothers. When Fancy saw him again Derek was atop The Bull's roof, hanging a huge sign that said, VOTE FRANK STANDISH FOR FREEDOM.

A tear welled in Fancy's eye as the sound of a single, wonderful word floated lightly, happily in her heart. The word was Mom.

***

Selby offered Frank a shot of scotch to calm his nerves, but he waved it away. Sharon massaged the cramps from his neck. Frank felt like he was about to charge a skirmish line. He lifted his eyes to the large white steer skull above the bar. He kissed his palm and slapped the bull head right between its big, empty eye sockets.

"Here goes nothing," said Frank. He turned to his friends and said, "Lord, give me strength." They clapped him on the back as he exited through the rear door and climbed the steps of the fire escape. He emerged onto the flat roof of The Bull to an explosion of cheers.

Twilight was dimming the suburban horizon as Frank leaned on his cane and gazed across the vast crowd, which anxiously simmered to a dull roar in anticipation of his Big Speech.

A chilly wind blew across his face. He felt a nervous flutter deep in his bowels, and a sharp pang of self-doubt ... *Frank, what have you gotten yourself into? You're not mayor material* ... And maybe that was true, he conceded. But that's also exactly the kind of claim the reverend would make, and Frank was not about to give that fat jackass the satisfaction. He clenched his teeth and embraced the moment.

"Thank you for coming," Frank said to the crowd, before he fully realized he had grabbed the microphone. The P.A. speakers popped with a brief squeal of feedback, but his words boomed clearly over the audience. People burst into hurrahs and shouts of support.

He cleared his throat, which felt sawdust dry. "My name is Frank Standish, and I'm campaigning to serve one single term as your mayor."

Again, the crowd erupted. Someone was blaring an air horn while others were blowing whistles among the patchwork of clapping and hooting.

"Thank you very much," Frank smiled broadly. "But y'all will have to settle down or this could take all night."

The audience laughed and gradually calmed.

"I'm not much of a politician," he said, looking over the hundreds of faces. "I've held a lot of jobs in my life, but I never had to get elected. So I doubt that what I have to say tonight will make a very professional political speech."

Frank realized he was tapping his cane as a nervous twitch, and he shoved his left hand over the other.

"To begin with, most politicians tell you that they're running for election with you in mind. They say that they represent your best interests. Don't they, Oscar?"

Oscar was standing proudly at the front of the crowd. "That's what they say!" he shouted back with gusto.

"That's what they say," echoed Frank loudly over the sound system. "My father had a word for what they say … that word is *HOGWASH!*"

The audience howled, jumping with excitement.

Frank continued, "I'm not going to lie to you good people. I believe doing so would be an insult to your intelligence. I'm going to level with you. To be completely honest, I'm here for my own interests. I'm here primarily for Frank Standish."

The crowd grew quiet with an awkward murmur that rippled through the hush.

"I'm here because I'm a hard-working, tax-paying, God-fearing, freedom-loving citizen of Fulton Springs who was born and raised here and who *will not* sit idly by while some corrupt politician *over-regulates* my business, *misspends* my tax dollars, *sells out* to special interests and *dictates* how I'll live my life!"

The response was deafening, backed by booming chants of *"Standish! Standish! Standish!"*

"Our mayor has painted me as a sinful man who wants nothing more in life than money and vice." Frank was hitting a stride, limping from one corner of the roof to the other, meeting as many eyes as he could. "Well, I showed up tonight to tell you that the mayor is a liar. Because what matters most to me is not money, beer or gambling … it's freedom! Freedom lets me earn my living as I see fit. Freedom lets me raise my family the way I think best. Freedom allows me to worship the way I choose to worship. And freedom is what guarantees that nobody can take those rights away from me. Any attack on my freedom is just that—an attack—and I've decided to fight back. Because when it comes to freedom and government, if you give them an inch, they'll take the whole damn city."

Intermittent shouts of approval shot from the crowd, and he had their rapt attention.

"I'm on the defense ... in defense of my freedom. The mayor flashes his Bible and claims I'm an evil man on T.V., and then he doesn't have the guts to show up tonight and defend those lies. Because he knows I'd defend myself by asking him a question that he couldn't answer. I'd ask him: 'Mayor, if I'm such an evil man, then where are all the victims of my evil deeds?'"

The crowd looked among themselves quizzically, considering the question.

"You see, there are no victims, because I mind my own business and would never dream of infringing on another individual's rights. The truth is that Mayor Cornelius and I simply have a different vision about the role government should play in our lives. I think government should protect our right to run our own lives. The Mayor thinks that government should run our lives.

"But that fundamental truth doesn't make a good campaign platform for the mayor, so he resorts to lies and distortions of my character.

"So, here's the deal. I'm no saint, and you may not like some of my personal decisions. For example, it is true that I serve beer in my restaurant. If that offends your delicate sensibilities, then I suggest you avoid the Bull and choose Momma Cooper's delicious soul food. If you don't like my smoking policy, then choose the Magnolia Café—or any one of our other fine Fulton Springs establishments. You see, the operative word is 'choose.' You have the right to choose where you dine just like I have a right to choose what I serve. That's the beauty of freedom.

"However …" Frank paused for dramatic effect. "Under the reign of the current mayor, all of our rights are under attack—the business owners' and the customers'. The mayor's new regulations determine the ingredients of the food I serve. Not only does this limit my freedom to run my business, but it limits your choices of what you can eat at your local restaurants. It seems to me that when it comes to what we eat—that's none of the mayor's cotton-picking business."

The crowd was back, cheering with support.

"As your mayor, I would never be so arrogant, so condescending, as to dictate to the voting public what they will or will not be allowed to eat. And while the mayor claims that these new laws are for 'your best interest' … Well, my father had a word that."

"HOGWASH!" sang the shouts of his supporters.

"The truth is that his new dietary regulations have nothing to do with your best interest. They have everything to do with the mayor's political future … Your mayor has been very comfortable in his position, just like a sow in the summer slop. He's grown accustomed to an uncontested election. When I came out of the woodwork, he got spooked. He had to throw together a campaign at any cost. And the cost was high. He promised a handful of special interest groups some powerful political favors in exchange for the mountain of cash it cost him to run those wall-to-wall campaign commercials.

"In a nutshell, his recent campaign has cost you your right to eat what you want, to fish where you want, and it's even cost you your constitutional right to bear arms—a decision that resulted in an immediate spike in crime and a physical attack on my family.

"So, while I doubt the mayor could bring forth a single victim of my *dastardly* ways, I can produce several victims of his policies, beginning with everyone who was robbed the night of his gun ban."

Frank had not prepared a formal speech. He had planned to speak from the heart, and completely off the cuff. As he did so, he found that his passions had a voice of their own, and the war-cry of his convictions had been waiting for release like a cork under pressure.

"And you want some more victims? Try every one of you, any Fulton Springs resident who pays taxes. Taxes are supposed to improve our city, for all of us. If they're being misallocated to benefit only a few select people, then I consider that to be theft, not fiscal responsibility. Do you realize that under the mayor's watch, local taxes have increased 14 times, in one form or another? Sales tax, property tax, business tax—you name it. That equates to hundreds of thousands of dollars. And in that time, we've seen no new public roads, parks or utilities. The only growth comes from private business at the new mall. Where do you suppose all the money is going? And all the while, the salaries of the mayor and his cronies have skyrocketed, more than doubling in just a few years.

"Simply put, the mayor is incrementally taking more and more money out of your pockets, and putting it into his own. And he's counting on your votes to keep the gravy train coming."

"*HOGWASH!*" cheered the crowd in refrain.

***

After the initial rush of traffic was halted by police and diverted from the park, the oncoming vehicles dwindled to a trickle. They finally stopped altogether. After a while, the only people occupying the premises were the police, and the park took on a conspicuous emptiness. The quiet inactivity troubled Officer Farling. Just as he began to sense a snag in the mayor's plan, his police radio crackled to life. He reached into his cruiser for the mic.

"Farling here. Please repeat."

"Farling, this is Jones. I was on patrol over by Main, and it looks like we've got a situation developing at The Bull restaurant. Send all available units."

"Copy that," he said, with his temper heating. "What's the nature of the situation?"

"I don't exactly know. But it's big," said Jones. "And loud."

"Dammit!" cursed Farling. He pounded the dashboard, reached across the console and chirped the siren to alert the officers across the park. He beckoned them with the swoop of an arm.

"What's going on?" asked Brookings.

"We're pulling out," said Farling through clenched teeth. "They've relocated."

***

When Pierce received news of the rally at The Bull, he was

prepared. He had anticipated just such a contingency and activated the troops he had on standby. Within a matter of moments a three-pronged battalion of concerned citizens descended on the gathering, armed with Cornelius reelection propaganda and a sense of righteous indignation. The insurgency consisted of members of Mother's Against Driving Drunk, the First Baptist Clean Living Women's Auxiliary, as well as a group of politically ambitious college interns posing as health food advocates.

"Re-elect the reverend! Re-elect the reverend!" chanted the Baptist women's contingent as they intermingled with the crowd, encouraging others to join their effort.

Unfazed, Frank continued his tirade.

***

"Freedom is what built this country and freedom is what'll keep it great," Frank said into the microphone. "But we've grown lazy as a people, and we accept limitations on our freedom without a fuss. When you allow the government to make decisions in your life, you are allowing them to control you. When someone controls you, you are not free. When someone controls you, you have a master." Frank pointed his cane at the crowd. "Who else in history had a master?"

He was impressed with his own stream of consciousness, and thought he was winging it rather well—so far.

"That's right, slaves had masters ... who else tries to dictate how other people live their lives? Dictators, that's who ... I'm perfectly capable of making decisions for myself, and I'm sure you people feel the same way. And that's why I'm running for mayor. I want to reintroduce real freedom to the people of Fulton Springs."

Applause sizzled through the audience, but one corner of the crowd grew shrill and hostile.

"We don't need drunkenness and irreverence here in Fulton Springs!" screeched a heavyset curly-haired woman wearing an overstretched T-shirt and waving a cardboard cross.

"Drunkenness and irreverence!" Frank smiled to the crowd. "It sounds like someone believes everything they see on TV. But that's okay, because this concerned lady brings me to my next point. You see, with freedom comes responsibility, and that's where the mayor says I'm a bad and sinful influence. The mayor doesn't seem to understand the concept that freedom must be coupled with responsibility. I believe a grown man should have the freedom to have a beer with his barbecue. I do not, however, condone drunken driving. Drunken driving can lead to car wrecks, which can kill people, damage property and generally rob the victims of the crash of their liberty in one way or another. And that liberty is a sacred thing to me—freedom is sacred, and must be protected. That's why we have stiff laws against drunk driving, which I will uphold. But I will not prohibit alcohol sales, which would amount to a preemptive punishment against all the other law-abiding adults who behave responsibly. You see how it works? We hold responsible parties accountable for their actions while preserving freedoms for the public at large. That's how I'll govern Fulton Springs if you elect me as mayor."

***

Mayor Davenport Cornelius was downright pickled when Farling phoned with word of the rally. The mayor was unsure if the weekend would involve him toasting his victory or drowning his sorrows, but he was determined to prepare for either circumstance. He instructed Farling to come pick him up and escort him to The Bull. If Farling was incapable of shutting Standish down as instructed, then by golly he would see to it himself. He did still run the place, after all.

"If you want something done right..." muttered the mayor as he climbed into Farling's cruiser.

Farling bit his lip. He appreciated the substantial salary and outlandish pension plan he had negotiated with the mayor, but he never much liked the man.

***

"Re-elect the reverend! Re-elect the reverend!" The refrain came from a handful of trendy young adults huddling on the sidewalk, near the East wall of The Bull. *"Healthy diet for healthy people! Healthy diet for healthy people!"* Frank had no way of knowing that this was Pierce Mathers' group of imported interns who were ineligible to vote in Fulton Springs, had no interest in dietary legislation and had scarfed down a mountain of greasy cheeseburgers en route to the event.

"When you allow the current mayor to tell you what to eat, under the pretense that the government knows what is best for your health," continued Frank, "you aren't just surrendering your freedom, you're also abdicating your responsibility. It's not the mayor's responsibility to make sure you eat healthy. That's your responsibility. It's the price of freedom, and I believe freedom is easily worth that price.

"And I'll tell you another thing … Call me old-fashioned, but I think a lot of things that are wrong with this world boil down to an abdication of personal responsibility. From absentee parents to crime and drug addiction. Keep that in mind the next time you're willing to abdicate your personal responsibility to the government. You'll be contributing to the epidemic."

***

"What the hell!" swore Farling, whose cruiser met an impenetrable grid of parked cars three blocks from The Bull. Two other cruisers pulled up behind him.

The mayor shook his head and clenched his fists. "I can't believe this, Farling. Your department completely dropped the ball! Things are entirely out of hand. This is mob rule!"

Farling did not reply. He exited the car, slamming the door. He stood on the bumper to survey the scene. At least a hundred unoccupied vehicles blanketed the streets for several blocks, leaving no hope of vehicle passage. He could see Standish campaign signs everywhere, and hanging from The Bull were the enormous red-and-white banners that his precinct had confiscated from the interstate highway. RESIST CONTROL, read one of them. Farling could barely comprehend the blatant disregard for authority. It must be some sort of mass hysteria, he thought. This widespread level of lawlessness in Fulton Springs was no doubt the depraved result of

Frank Standish's unwholesome influence.

"Ticket 'em all!" Farling shouted to the other officers.

"Which ones, sir?"

"All of 'em. Cite them all."

"Yes, sir. But that could take all night—"

"CITE THEM ALL!" screamed Farling, ripping open the door to the cruiser. "Come on, Mayor," he barked into the car. "We take the rest on foot."

The mayor grabbed the police bullhorn from the floorboard and followed Farling into the crowd.

***

"Let's be honest about the motivations for these limits that are put on our freedom," Frank said. "New laws that restrict what you can eat aren't introduced for your benefit, they're introduced for the law-makers' benefit. The mayor doesn't really care what you eat. He only cares about catering to whatever special interest groups bring him money and votes. If that happens to be food regulators, so be it. He needs the money and votes to remain in office, which gives him the power to barter away more of your freedoms for more money and votes. As long as there's another election to win, the song remains the same.

"These days it seems like practically every politician sells out the principles they claim to hold during their campaign. They do it for one reason: to guarantee their reelection. They give political favors to all sorts of special interests, and these groups in turn contribute money or guarantee voter turnout at the ballot box. The job ceases to be about philosophy or principles, and instead becomes about selfishness. In many ways, it boils down to simple bribery," said Frank. "Whether it's legal or not, I think it's wrong. And it's not the way our government was meant to work.

"Look, I'm sure that the power and influence of public office can give someone a really prestigious feeling. I'm sure that after someone gets used to that, it can be tough to give it up. But when the person holding that position is willing to sacrifice the freedoms of his constituents in exchange for another term in office, then that person is no longer serving the people, he's serving only himself.

"And that's where I come in," Frank limped from one corner of the roof to the other, his cane clicking with each step. "I plan to serve only one term. I'm a barbecue man at heart, and that's where I want to stay. The city was interfering with my barbecue business, so I've got to take a little detour and serve as mayor, so I can get them off my back and go back to work in peace.

"And there's a good reason I'm so adamant about serving only one-term. Because I want it to serve as a promise to the public. With no chance of a second term, you can be guaranteed that I will not surrender to temptation—the temptation to sell out the interests of the city in return for more political power. I have no further political ambition. I'll not be seeking any more power. I'm imposing my own strict term limit. I'll use my time to roll back the mayor's latest business regulations and lifestyle restrictions. I don't want the city telling me how to run my restaurant. I won't tell you what to do, either.

"I plan to restore fiscal responsibility to city government just like I keep the books for my business—with a balanced budget and an eye on the bottom line. I'll also level the playing field for private businesses by instituting an open-bid process for public contracts.

And I'll keep the city's business a matter of public record, so the people of Fulton Springs will always know who's bending my ear. Most of all, I'll do whatever I can to protect your rights and property. Let's keep Fulton Springs a nice place to live and a safe place to raise a family."

Frank had not convinced the entire crowd to support his candidacy, but he had won enough people to drown out his few detractors with a cheerful, glorious racket that echoed throughout the city streets.

***

While Frank was speaking, Farling and the mayor had been wrestling their way through the densely packed crowd to the metal staircase, at the rear of the building, that lead to the roof. Farling climbed up first. The mayor was huffing and puffing at the rear, finding the stairs to be a vexing physical hurdle.

When Farling reached the top, he saw just how far the crowd stretched, and how many citizens were rooting for Standish, as though he were some cult icon with legions of fans. But Standish was no politician, thought Farling. And he was no figure of authority. He was just an average nobody. What could they possibly see in him?

"Standish!" he shouted. "What the hell are you doing? Get down from this roof!"

Frank squinted to make out Officer Farling standing outside the glow of the work lamps that were used to illuminate The Bull's makeshift stage.

"Well, well," Frank said into the mic. "It looks like I've got some company up here on the roof."

The booming command of Frank's electronically amplified voice sounded incredibly powerful compared to his own, and Farling felt emasculated.

"Stand down, Standish!" he hissed. "Stop this crap! Get over here or I'll arrest you for inciting a riot!"

Frank turned to the audience. "There's a police officer lurking up here in the shadows. He says I should stand down. He says I should call it quits or he's going to arrest me for inciting a riot."

Many in the crowd responded with boos and hisses. Farling felt betrayed. He was entitled to their support. He was the law. It was his job, his duty, to restore order.

"But I don't see any riot," continued Frank. "All I see is the good people of Fulton Springs. We were planning to peacefully assemble at the public park, but you stopped us all from doing so, Officer Farling."

Shouts of solidarity came from the audience. Farling bit his lip. He stepped into the light. "What you're doing is illegal!" he shouted.

"These people came to listen to the candidates for mayor," said Frank as he turned to Farling. "They're here, they're civil, they're peaceful. It's not my fault only one of the candidates showed up. But we're here now. And if you try to shut us down, then it won't be me who starts a riot ..."

"Let him talk!" came from the crowd. *"Get lost, Farling!"* *"Let Standish speak!"* Voices from every corner were sounding off like a chorus of angry crickets.

Farling trembled with fury. He wanted to draw his baton and crack Frank across the teeth. He wanted to knock him to the ground and thrash his skull with the club, again and again. He might have done it, too, if not for a thousand eyes witnessing his every move. Those eyes were the town, his neighbors, and ultimately his employers. As top cop, he was supposed to be a respected figure in the community, but here he was facing down a new local hero. He had somehow found himself in the role of the villain.

"I don't believe I will stand down, officer," said Frank. "Today, I think I'll stand up. And I think you should stand down."

Farling knew if he cuffed Standish for arrest, there was a strong likelihood that his most rabid supporters would physically intervene. Although he had the law on his side, they definitely had the numbers. Things could get ugly. On the other hand, to do nothing was to display impotence and concede that the city's laws no longer ruled the day. If that was the case, then his role as an enforcement officer was a useless one, and he might never regain the respect of the citizens. He had a choice to make: the plank or the noose.

***

"Things are really heating up now, folks!" said Mad Marty Madigan to his radio audience. He and Vanessa had set up a broadcast table in plain sight and earshot of The Bull's roof. "The authorities have arrived and are attempting to shut things down. And Standish appears to be resisting!"

He noticed Vanessa beckoning to someone in the crowd. Daphne Shields and the Community Heartbeat Crew rushed to the table.

"Hey Marty, Hey V," said Daphne, half out of breath. "What'd I miss so far?"

"Good stuff. Standish is on a roll, but the cops just showed!"

"You're kidding!" she said.

Her videographer, Greg Iris, raised his camera like a cannon for battle.

"We saw the mayor pass by, too," said Vanessa. "Sparks are gonna fly!"

Daphne literally squealed with excitement. "I've gotta run!" she said, and the Community Heartbeat team darted into the crowd.

***

Farling felt perspiration beading on his brow. He was trying to keep his cool, but he felt the weight of all the eyes on him, awaiting his next move. He felt like he was in a gunfight showdown in an old western movie, and that he was wearing the black hat. *Where had things gone so wrong?*

"TOTAL DEFIANCE OF LAW AND ORDER!" bellowed the voice of the reverend from the shadows. "TOTAL CHAOS and COMPLETE DISORDER!" The mayor was shouting into a bullhorn to compete with Frank's P.A. system.

The mayor stepped into the orange light of the lamps. His tie was askew and his red face was wet with sweat. He was greeted with a spattering of applause followed by a few approving shouts from his devout parishioners. Most of the audience was silent.

The mayor's appearance was a great relief for Farling. He had frozen in the limelight; it was burning him alive. He took the opportunity to make as graceful an exit as he thought possible. With the mayor drawing all the attention, Farling wordlessly retreated to the shadows and slunk off the roof into obscurity.

"TOTAL DISREGARD FOR LAW AND ORDER—that's exactly what you can expect from a city run by Frank Standish!" screamed the mayor from the rooftop.

A small chirp of cheers was shrouded in a cascade of boos and angry retorts.

"Simply look around and bear witness to his influence," said Cornelius through his bullhorn. "This is the center of town! This mob behavior is utter lawlessness! This cannot be tol—"

The mayor's words were lost to a great mechanical roar that seemed to shake the heavens like the wail of a titan. Frank waved his hand broadly in the air and slid it across his throat in a gesture to cease. The clamor subsided. The noise had come from the Butler Brothers and their biker friends revving their engines to smother the reverend's message.

"I appreciate the gesture, boys," said Frank to the bikers. "But let's listen to what the mayor has to say. I want to extend him the courtesy that he would not grant to any of us."

***

Pierce Mathers felt compelled to watch the drama unfold. He recognized that the mayor's decision to confront Standish was a terrible idea, and had said so. But the mayor had been deaf to his protests, possessed by hubris and a demanding sense of entitlement. The mayor's flailing attempts to neutralize his opponent had run out of time. Frank Standish was now overseeing a massive revival of civic pride, and the voters would cast their ballots in the morning. It was obvious who owned the momentum, and that harsh reality was too much for the mayor to idly bear. So rather than completely avoid confrontation as according to plan, Cornelius had felt railroaded into a desperate public plea to salvage votes, and was forced to do so on Frank's home field. It was a tactical nightmare, and Pierce expected a spectacular failure of mythic proportions. Sure, the mayor's political influence—and Pierce's fast-track career trajectory—was going up in flames, but at the very least Pierce felt he deserved to behold the fiery pageantry. He elbowed his way through the crowd and positioned himself at the front and center of the Fulton Springs audience, just in time for Rev. Dave to make his bombastic appearance.

***

"Sin and iniquity!" preached the reverend, pointing at Frank. "That's what this man will bring to our fine city! Beware the high cost of low living! When he uses words like 'freedom,' he's speaking in code. When he wants 'freedom,' he really wants more *booze*. When he says 'freedom,' he wants the freedom *to gamble. To sin!* Do not be fooled by this wolf in sheep's clothing!

"I'm here to tell you, Mr. Standish ... The Lord is watching us all. You'd better change your direction, or you're gonna end up right where you're going!" Cornelius waved his finger at the sky emphatically.

Frank wanted a cigarette.

"The Lord has watched o'er Fulton Springs during my tenure as mayor," said Cornelius. "He has treated us like a coddled child. He has been at our side from our modest beginnings and walked with us as we've flourished into an expanding business community. The Lord has been with us, and now we're in high cotton, seein' progress like never before. Don't turn your back on Christ almighty by usherin' in this heathen dealer of liquor and cigarettes. What kind of gratitude would that be? How would that thank the Lord for his many blessings?"

Frank spoke into the mic: "This man wants to control what you drink, what you eat, how you live, and then he picks your pocket. If that's what you call holy, then I ain't holy."

"This man," spat the mayor, pointing to himself, "has to govern. It's my job. It's what I was elected to do ... Something you don't know anything about, Standish! Rules are required to maintain order. Laws! Systems that keep the city under control!"

"You want the city under *your* control," said Frank. "But we don't need you telling us what to do. I know what's better for me and my family than you do. And so do these people."

Many in the crowd raised their voices in support.

"You have no idea what it takes to run a city," said the mayor. "What you're advocating is lawlessness."

"No, I don't want lawlessness. I want restraint. I don't want to eliminate government, I want to limit it. You want to grow it, because it gives you more power. And that's where I've got a problem."

"The city needs a leader," screamed Cornelius. "Not a bartender!"

"For the most part, people can lead themselves," said Frank. "We're talking about grown adults, Reverend. We're not stupid, and you aren't as smart as you think you are. Responsible adults don't need a babysitter. We want the government off our backs so we can get busy leading our lives without any hassle. You want to micro-manage everyone, and then expect to be thanked for it with another term in office. People are waking up, mayor. They're tired of that crap. And I believe your days of playing king are slimmin' down like a bride to be."

The crowd was energetic. Somewhere toward the center of the swarm, the mayor heard a voice shouting for his attention. It was Pierce Mathers. *"Mayor!"* he shouted. *"Bring up the arrest! Hit him on the drugs!"*

Fuel to the fire, thought Mathers from his 50-yard line vantage point.

"You talk a big game, Mr. Standish," said the reverend into his bullhorn. "But how in the world are you going to preside over an entire city, when you can't even keep your own house in order? I mean, drugs? That's not a minor traffic offense that your son was charged with. He lives under your roof, and he was caught in possession of illegal narcotics."

"My son is not running for mayor. I am." Frank knew the reverend's charge was damaging. Fulton Springs was largely an old-fashioned town with socially conservative values. The drug allegation, even for something like marijuana, seen by many cultures as harmless and commonplace, would strike many local voters as an unforgivable indiscretion, up there with crack cocaine and horse molestation. Unfortunately for Frank, a great many people bought into a simple rule of thumb: If it is illegal, it must be evil. The charge would be seen as a poor reflection of the Standish name.

"Your son's arrest speaks not only about the character of your son, but to the unseemly environment that you foster in your home. This is the South, Mr. Standish. You're the man of the house. Do you not assume responsibility for what takes place beneath your roof?"

"Of course I do," said Frank. "But my son is a grown man and can take responsibility for his own actions."

"I see. So you're saying it's not your fault ..." The mayor turned to the crowd with an exaggerated shrug of the shoulders and a knowing wink. "That sounds exactly like a man running for office."

Nice blow, thought Mathers, cracking his knuckles down in the crowd. He was surprised the mayor had it in him.

***

Derek was agonizing over the fact that his arrest had given Cornelius his most dangerous ammunition. He knew the concept of drug use was an emotional trigger for many voters in Fulton Springs, prone to react instinctively with revulsion and fear. They had seen TV commercials where marijuana users drove their cars over children on tricycles. They were terrified that such a social plague might overtake the cul-de-sacs of their fine city. Still, it felt unfair for his father to take the heat. It was Derek's crime—his "sin"—and it should bear no reflection on his father, but he realized many voters would feel differently.

"What this tells us," continued the reverend. "Is that Frank Standish is one of two people. He's either a man who's too incompetent to successfully manage his home in a morally upstanding manner. Or, he's a man who tolerates illicit drug use. Either way, we don't need him in office, whether he's incompetent ... or an accessory to criminal activity."

The mayor knew he had struck a soft spot in light of the crowd's restrained reaction. The people were unsure of the validity of the charges, but the allegation did not bode well for Frank. The hooting and hollering had subsided, and the people were nearly silent. The anticipation for Frank's reply was palpable.

He glassed Cornelius from head to toe. Back in his youthful days, Frank might have considered the mayor's mouthing to be fist-fighting words. Even at his current ripe age, he secretly wanted to knock him out. Instead, Frank would have to respond civilly, intelligently and honestly, recognizing his responsibility as a role model to his son and admitting some degree of failure for his son's poor decision. He raised the mic, but as he drew it to his lips he saw a figure appear at the edge of the pool of light. When he recognized the face, he lowered the mic.

Edna Standish walked slowly into the orange glow and smiled at Frank. "Hi, son."

Frank was stunned. It made no sense that his sickly mother should appear on the roof of The Bull during his contentious confrontation with the mayor. It was surreal.

"I need this," she said, reaching for the microphone. She wore a light green robe and a scarf on her head. Frank handed her the cord.

The mayor was as confused as Frank.

"Hello," she said to the crowd, her voice soft and unassuming. "My name is Edna Standish. I'm Frank's mom."

The audience was perplexed, but after a moment of silence they offered her a round of respectful applause.

"I'm sure I'm not supposed to be here right now. But I had something important to say," said Edna, her words modest and measured. Frank detected a subtle hitch in her voice and the glisten of a tear in her eye, and it tortured him. "In fact, I guess you'd call it a confession."

With one hand she reached up and unwrapped the white scarf from her head. It unfolded in a broad spiral swath, and revealed the ghost-pale skin of her scalp with only a few wisps of silky white hair.

170

"I've heard all the talk about my grandson. All the allegations. Well, I'm here to tell you that it's all a bunch of ... well, it's a bunch of hogwash," she grinned at Frank.

"You see, I'm sick. I'm fighting breast cancer. I'm not here for your sympathy, but I will say that cancer is a cruel disease, and if you've ever experienced it within your family, then you know how bad things can get. And sometimes I feel like the treatment is as bad as the disease."

Frank began to mist and made a valiant effort not to cry

"Chemotherapy ..." she said. "Chemo is a pretty harsh treatment with a lot of nasty side effects. It causes nausea and vomiting and all sorts of aches and pains. I don't mean to whine, but it's a real bear to deal with. And, one day in one of my support groups a fellow patient told me a secret that helped her cope with the side effects. I was shocked at first. She said she smoked marijuana. A hippie, I thought, because that's what I had been trained to think. But then I got sicker and sicker. It got so bad that I could not eat, and I could not keep anything down when I *could* eat. I was miserable. I got desperate. And I tried it ... marijuana," said Edna. "What can I say? It worked."

The mayor was flabbergasted. Everyone in attendance was engrossed in the woman's story, completely icing his hot streak. And pushing her off the roof was probably a bad idea.

Frank was dumbfounded as well. He knew his mother had been suffering, but Edna went to great lengths to protect her son from the gory details of the disease, knowing how deeply it stung him. She refused to be a burden. She was a good mother, first and foremost, and a strong, independent woman who did not care much for whiners.

"When I smoked it, I could eat without vomiting," she

continued, "which helped me get back some of my strength. And it lessened the pain. Basically, it helped me regain some quality of life. Sure, I knew it was illegal, but I didn't feel that what I was doing was wrong. Anything that stopped the pain was a welcome relief. When you're in a situation where you're in constant pain and discomfort, your perspective on life tends to change a bit. I could not understand why it was illegal. Whether or not my only source of relief was kosher in the eyes of the law—well, that didn't seem like a very pertinent issue in the grand scheme of things ... One thing became clear: The people who are always clamoring to keep medical marijuana illegal, those people aren't cancer patients."

She draped the scarf back over her head and continued, "I feel that my real mistake was involving my grandson in an illegal activity. He discovered I was using it as medication. He knew I was having a difficult time acquiring it. He saw that it brought me relief and stepped in to help me keep it in stock. Derek, my grandson, he doesn't even smoke the stuff. He was only trying to help me, and he went to jail for his effort. And I feel absolutely awful about that. I'm so sorry, Derek."

Deep in the crowd, Derek was hanging on every word, his heart wrenching with her story.

Frank was frozen. The revelations poured over him like a flood from a breeched levy.

"That's what I wanted to clear up. The mayor can prattle about my son and my grandson all he wants, but he doesn't have a lick of credibility," said Edna, her voice taking a sharper tone. "Here's the truth: I have cancer, so I use medical marijuana. I'm at peace with the Lord Jesus Christ about my decision, and I don't much care what anyone else thinks of me.

"But I do care what people think of my family. Yes, my

grandson was supplying cannabis for me. So, he may have done something illegal, but I don't feel he did anything wrong. He only wanted to help his sick grandma. And my son, Frank, he's a good man and a fine father. He makes an excellent role model. He didn't raise some hooligan. He raised a caring and compassionate son, someone who would do whatever it takes to help his grandmother."

She stood on her toes and kissed Frank's cheek, hugging his waist. Miraculously, he kept his composure.

She turned back to the audience. "I think Frank Standish is exactly the kind of man that Fulton Springs needs as mayor."

Edna lowered the mic. She handed it to Frank and quietly stepped into the shadows, leaving Frank and the reverend staring eye to eye.

The mayor immediately stepped away, addressing the hushed audience. "Well, well, well," said Cornelius into his bullhorn. "What you have just witnessed simply proves my point. We have a whole family—*three generations!*—who feel they can simply live above the law, as though it does not apply to them the way it does to the rest of us. Well, that's not the way a city works. We have rules to live by and—"

"Shut up, mayor," said Frank. "You've talked about my family enough." He walked to the reverend and plucked the bullhorn from his hands. Frank went to the rear wall and chucked it into the dumpster, to the delight of the audience.

"Time to wrap this up," Frank said to the masses, the P.A. crackling with feedback. "For the record, I'll stand behind my family through thick and thin. I'm proud of my mother; she's a saint among sinners. And I'm proud of my son. Maybe prouder than ever." He wiped his eye. "He's got heart and he's got guts."

Derek choked up. At that moment he felt an unbreakable bond

with his father. They shared not only love and blood but a fundamental philosophy. They believed that every man gets just one shot at life, and it's a gift to use wisely. They both believed a man's got to decide for himself what is right and wrong in the world. He must decide for himself what the truth is. And he's got to spend his life making decisions based on what he thinks is right and wrong, not just adopting the ideas that others think are right or wrong. At that moment they both felt that bonding spirit, they recognized it in each other, but they would never speak of it openly.

"Go get 'em, Pop!" Derek shouted from the mob through cupped hands. *"Vote for Standish!"*

"Now, here's what you can tell your friends," Frank continued from the roof, his voice rising in strength. "When it comes to my candidacy as mayor, it's not about power, it's about the people. It's not about rules and regulations, it's about liberty. I want you to trust me with one term, and I'll do my best to run this city with those guiding principles. If you want bigger government, less freedom and higher taxes, then reelect the mayor. But if you want *less* government, *more* freedom and *lower* taxes, vote for Frank Standish.

"And I've got one last thing to say to you, Mayor." Frank took a step toward him, looking him dead in the eye.

The mayor was a sweaty mess of drunken dejection. He was fretting and fidgeting like a kid who needed to pee. Things had not gone according to plan. Frank had stolen his voice and thrown it in the trash, and there was nowhere left to turn. He was at a total loss for the next move to make, and his sagging face exposed a man in the throes of defeat.

"You're on private property," Frank told the mayor. "Get the hell off my roof."

***

Pierce Mathers had watched from below, highly entertained by the theater of it all. He found himself surrounded with a thunder of cheers and shouts from Standish's growing army of supporters. He felt alone with his joylessness. You win some, you lose some, he thought with a shrug. Pierce took consolation in the fact that, although Cornelius was ready for the glue factory, he was still a young man and would pull through the election largely unscathed, regardless of the mayoral race ... even if he was stuck working with a barbecue salesman at city hall.

Pierce threw his coat over his shoulder and shoved through the crowd in search of any bar other than The Bull.

***

Frank retired to the office of The Bull. As soon as he had a moment to himself, the pent-up emotion of all that had happened hit him like a foul ball in the blinding sun. He collapsed in his chair and his vision clouded with tears. He grabbed a tissue, wiped his eyes and immediately heard a rap at the office door. He instantly dammed up the oncoming gusher.

Fancy pushed opened the door and smiled. "My hero," she said. She sat in his lap and hugged him. Nora appeared at his side and did the same.

Then Derek stepped into the doorway.

Frank looked up and gave him a deferential nod. "Looks like I owe you an apology."

Derek shook his head. "No, you don't," he said. "But I'll be looking for an acceptance speech."

Frank's mother appeared behind Derek. Rocky showed up behind Edna. Nathan Stevenson, Sharon McClendon, Oscar and Selby appeared. Marty Madigan, Daphne Shields, Fred Matthews, the Butlers, the Ortiz brothers, Momma Cooper's crew and the owners of The Magnolia—all the old regulars and lots of new friends began to populate the restaurant.

Within minutes, The Bull became host to the biggest party Fulton Springs had ever seen. The energy and excitement were irresistible. The revelers enjoyed music and dancing and laughing deep into the morning.

***

No one else knew it, but Mayor Davenport Cornelius never actually left the roof of The Bull that night, as Frank had instructed. The mayor hated being told what to do. He stood trembling in the shadows until the mass of people in the streets finally dispersed. He was exhausted. He kneeled onto the dirty asphalt sheeting and rolled forward, flopping onto his side in the fetal position and curling his coat around him. He wanted to move away to another town and never see any of those people again.

A few moments later the roof began to vibrate with the bass beats of the party music below. He rolled onto his back and gazed into the heavens. It was a cool, clear night and thousands of stars sparkled in the sky. The reverend asked God why He had forsaken him. He waited patiently for an answer, sobbing like a child, and eventually fell asleep. He never got a reply. God did not want to be bothered.

***

The polls opened the next morning at six, and the town was bustling with the election drama. Throughout the day, phone-captured videos from the rally at The Bull appeared all over the internet. Marty Madigan's radio coverage of the rally was re-broadcast due to popular demand.

The ballot officials reported a very healthy voter turnout, inspired by Frank's fresh wave of support, as well as a strong contingent of the reverend's faithful followers, who either saw Frank as a minion of the devil or they simply recognized that their status as prime beneficiaries of the city's sweetheart deals might soon cease to exist. A line of people could be seen wrapping around the designated voting location, the Fulton Springs Public Library, until late in the afternoon. The polls remained busy until voting closed at seven in the evening.

Frank was mopping the floor of The Bull after the dinner rush when Nathan Stevenson brought news that the results were final. It had been a tight race, but Frank had won the election by a slim margin. In one month, he would assume office, and Rev. Davenport Cornelius would be forced to step down.

Frank absorbed the news steadily. He had expected a close race, since most of the mayor's base would have avoided Frank's impromptu rally, but had felt optimistic for a victory since witnessing the mania of the previous evening.

Frank was not the only winner. Nathan Stevenson and Rocky Jones had unseated two of the four-member city council. Pierce Mathers and one of the First Baptist deacons were still on the rolls, but Frank would serve as the tie-breaker on any contentious issues of city planning.

With all the changes among city officials, things were already looking up for the freedoms of Fulton Springs.

***

Within a week after he took office, Matilda was back at home beneath The Bull's bar top. The citizens were no longer disarmed by decree. The Catholic Senior Citizens Club was free to resume its weekly bingo games. The fishing ban at Six Mile Creek was completely eliminated, spunks be damned. The mayor's dietary regulations on sugar, salt and trans-fat were discontinued. The people of Fulton Springs were free to eat what they wanted, and were expected to be responsible for their own nutritional health. Restaurants were free to implement smoking and non-smoking sections into their businesses, as they saw fit, without fear of fine or other legal reprisal.

Within two weeks, Barry Finkelstein got his pot-hole filled.

Frank decided to quit smoking. It was a personal decision based on a strong desire to stick around for his family and maybe even hug a grandchild one day. He dropped the habit cold turkey. Had he been compelled to stop smoking at the behest of some bureaucrat, he would never have given up the cigarettes.

Officer Farling transferred to another precinct to avoid working with the new mayor. Frank immediately appointed Art Brookings, a man he knew to be honest, evenhanded and just, to serve as police chief.

Whenever in office, Frank maintained an open-door policy to the public. The monthly city council meetings were conducted as informal free-spoken forums, where engaged citizens aired their concerns and openly exchanged ideas. They appreciated the genuine, attentive feedback they got from Frank, Nathan and Rocky. There was, of course, disagreement with some of the constituents, but Frank never wavered in principle.

"I'm sick and tired of the smoking at Miss Cooper's restaurant," complained Velma Loudermilk, a bespectacled school teacher who thought the world needed more rules. "They shouldn't be allowed to have a smoking section. In fact, selling cigarettes shouldn't even be allowed in the city!"

Frank explained that Velma was free to avoid Momma Copper's place, and was in no way forced to purchase cigarettes.

"I know that!" Velma would say. "But what if I want to eat at Cooper's!"

"You're free to do that, ma'am."

"But people are smoking there!" she wailed.

"That may be true," said Frank. "You're free not to go, if that bothers you."

And so it went.

The city was contractually obligated to fulfill the business dealings Cornelius had set up in his administration, but no further public contracts were awarded unless they first passed an open-bid process before the council chambers—and anyone in town was welcome to watch and comment on the proceedings.

As the new shopping center opened, Frank slashed the city's sales tax rate. Not only did this allow the residents to keep more of their earnings when shopping in town, but the measure attracted customers from surrounding cities who could shop Fulton Springs with more buying power than in the other retail communities competing nearby with higher tax rates.

The resulting economic surge resulted in greater overall tax revenue than previous years, and the city's first priority was to allocate the available funds for the purchase of the long-promised computer systems for the Fulton Springs elementary school.

Derek Standish was held legally accountable for possession of an illegal substance. However, after hearing Edna Standish's admission at the The Bull that night, Judge Roper suspended the sentence and directed him to a court-referral program where Derek had to pee in a cup every two weeks and attend a weekly Narcotics Anonymous class. Although it beat a stint in jail, the routine lasted six months and was an extraordinary waste of time for a young man who did not use drugs.

During that time, Derek continued to provide his grandmother with medical marijuana, despite her protests. He would sneak it over, slip it into her refrigerator and never mention a word about it. He did this despite his personal risk of legal consequences. In his view, his crime harmed no one but helped someone. If he were to cease doing it, then his grandmother would be denied her medication and suffer more severely from the disease. He was not about to let that happen, so Derek continued his sinister activity and never gave a damn what anyone else thought about the matter. After a year, Edna's cancer went into remission and her health improved substantially. Soon, she was no longer in need of the medicine, and Derek's job was over.

Despite all odds, Derek did discover one bright ray of sun under the glum cloud of the compulsory narcotics meetings. He met a girl. Her name was Sarah Eastman. She had pink hair, a witty sense of humor, and a smile that made Derek feel like he should comb his hair. The court had ordered her to attend the group sessions after she was caught fermenting and bottling her own wine—a flagrant violation of state law. When Derek found out she was the drummer for an all-girl punk rock band, he fell madly in love.

***

Despite their different interests and diverging obligations, Frank's family maintained a tradition of meeting each Sunday for dinner. They gathered in the afternoon, sometimes for potluck, but more often to cook together from scratch as a kind of fellowship activity. Frank and Derek would oversee the main course; Edna, Fancy and Sarah handled all the baking and desserts. Nora was in charge of icing all cakes and taste-testing the batter.

It was gumbo night, and Frank was rounding the table, serving everyone a steaming scoop from a wooden ladle. The scent of cayenne, shrimp, sausage and tomatoes enriched the air with a mouth-watering aroma. The girls had baked a broccoli-cheddar casserole, cornbread, and a monstrous pot of stewed collard greens. Blackberry cobbler was cooling on the window sill for dessert.

Everyone sat around the table and bowed their heads as Nora blessed the food.

"God is Great, God is Good, Let us thank Him for our food," she recited.

These moments were always the highlight of Frank's week.

"How are the greens?" asked Fancy.

"Mmmmm," grunted Frank with his mouth full, giving a thumbs-up.

"Nora, are you excited about the cobbler?" asked Edna.

Nora was wearing her tortoise costume from the school play. "Yes, Grandma, and I'll be needing some whip cream with it."

"How's the soup?" asked Frank.

"It's great, Pop," said Derek. "Spicy. Just the way I like it."

"It's really good, Mr. Standish" said Sarah, wiping the corner of her mouth with a napkin. "I think this is the one."

"Frank," he corrected, winking at Sarah. He had been experimenting with new recipes for his big comeback to the restaurant business, and she had been serving as his cooking apprentice. He planned to expand the menu a little beyond barbecue with some finely crafted staples of southern cuisine, and the gumbo was a front-runner.

"That's right," said Fancy, blowing her spoon to cool it off. "Pretty soon it's back to The Bull full time."

"Any news on who might be running for mayor?" asked

Edna. Her prognosis was sunny and it showed in her eyes. Her face glowed with renewed color and spirit, and she sipped heartily from the soup.

"Are you running for mayor, Daddy?" asked Nora.

"Not me," said Frank, shoveling down some casserole. The new family cat, which Nora had named Silver, curled around his leg. The cat had become a household fixture, and Frank was amazed how well it got along with the family dog.

"Not him," said Derek, sipping a glass of Sarah's homemade muscadine wine. "Dad promised not to run. Not that it matters ... I'll bet he still wins."

Frank shot him a sideways glance.

Derek shrugged. "Let's face it, there's always the write-in ballot."

THE END

NOTES & ACKNOWLEDGEMENTS

Thanks to **The Matt Murphy Show** *in Birmingham, Alabama, where I stole the saying, "Every man deserves to go to hell in his own fashion."*

Thanks to radio personality Richard Dixon, from whom I lifted the expression, "like a pit bull on a toddler."

Special thanks to Nancy D. Wall for the helpful copyediting.

And good luck to John Douglas, a real life Frank Standish in his own right.

In the short time since I released the first edition of THE BULL, the Alabama Homebrew Bill passed into law, which made it legal for citizens of the state to legally home-brew beer and wine. (Making moonshine is still illegal.) This bill succeeded in large part due to the efforts of the non-profit, grassroots organization Free the Hops (www.freethehops.org). Frank Standish can now make his wine without threat of incarceration.

However, it's not all good news in Alabama. Senate Bill 96 became law, which gives cities the power to decide what is in the public interest, and allows them to use eminent domain for "public and private" uses such as car plants, airplane manufacturers and more. This could make it easier for city officials to kick a guy like Oscar Stonewall out of his home. The new law allows cities to take property not only to benefit the health and welfare of the community, but to turn it over to private businesses.

— M.W.

www.ingramcontent.com/pod-product-compliance
Lightning Source LLC
Chambersburg PA
CBHW060155130626
46556CB00006B/2647